HIS SUBMISSIVE JEWEL

The Martinis and Chocolate Book Club 3

Lara Valentine

EVERLASTING CLASSIC

Siren Publishing, Inc.
www.SirenPublishing.com

A SIREN PUBLISHING BOOK
IMPRINT: Everlasting Classic

HIS SUBMISSIVE JEWEL
Copyright © 2013 by Lara Valentine

ISBN: 978-1-62242-760-4

First Printing: February 2013

Cover design by Les Byerley
All art and logo copyright © 2013 by Siren Publishing, Inc.

Printed in the U.S.A.

PUBLISHER
Siren Publishing, Inc.
www.SirenPublishing.com

HIS SUBMISSIVE JEWEL

The Martinis and Chocolate Book Club 3

LARA VALENTINE
Copyright © 2013

Chapter One

Noelle Carter was seriously screwed. What had seemed like a simple, no-big-deal thunderstorm earlier had turned into a nasty and possibly dangerous situation. Her impetuous and slightly stubborn nature had once again got her in trouble. She should have pulled off the road hours ago when she saw the weather change. But no, she stubbornly stuck to her schedule, determined to make her destination tonight. Now she would probably spend the night on the side of the road.

Noelle navigated her Honda Accord at a snail's pace up the deserted, rutted road. She strained to see through the sheets of rain obscuring her vision. The windshield wipers were going as fast as they could, but made little difference. The visibility was terrible, and she was afraid she was going to drive right off the road. She had long past left the streetlights of civilization behind and was now gripping her steering wheel with white knuckles, fighting the whipping wind determined to veer her off to the side of the road.

According to the map her sister, Abby, had provided her, the destination should be just about forty miles ahead. Noelle had been driving for three days from her home in Florida to this remote area of Montana for her little sister's wedding, and she was exhausted, hungry, and a little cranky.

Abby had fallen in love with a young man whose family owned a ranch, and the wedding would be held there. Noelle had agreed to come out ahead of the rest of the family to help with the arrangements. She had also designed the wedding rings for the couple. Thankfully, they were tucked safely away in her luggage in the backseat of the car. She hoped the couple would be as happy with them as she was. The set was some of her best work as a jewelry designer.

Her shoulders ached with tension and fatigue, and her stomach rumbled with hunger. She had been driving since early this morning, and she prayed her journey was hopefully near its end. When it was clear the weather was taking a turn for the worse, Noelle had called Abby to tell her she might be delayed. Abby had tried to convince her to pull over for the night, but so close to her destination, Noelle couldn't fathom stopping. She was cursing herself now. She could barely see two feet in front of the car.

Headlights in the distance had Noelle inching her car to the right, stopping on what she hoped was the shoulder. The last thing she wanted was a collision if she was over the center line. Or the center of the road, since there were no lines painted on this practically dirt road. She watched as an SUV slowed down as it neared her. She couldn't see the driver, but the vehicle was one of those Land Rovers that could handle these rough roads. The Rover passed her but quickly turned around and pulled up beside her. She breathed a sigh of relief, hoping the driver might tell her where she could pull over for the night. She rolled down her window as the driver did the same. For one moment, every horror film she'd ever seen flashed before her eyes. Getting into a car with, or even just talking to, a complete stranger on a dark, deserted road seemed a dumb thing to do, no matter what the weather was.

It was a dark and stormy night...

She giggled at her flight of fancy. She should be more serious, but it wasn't in her nature. She could see the humor in just about any situation.

"Noelle? Noelle Carter? Your sister, Abby, sent me to get you."

Thank you, Abby.

She could barely hear the voice of the driver, muffled by the driving rain, but if he knew her name it ruled out psychopathic killer pretty quick. She waved and called back, the rain getting in the window and soaking her and the seat.

"Yes! Yes, I'm Noelle!"

"I'll come out and help you into the car. Just give me a minute."

"You'll get soaked. I'll just hop up in the passenger seat from here. Just open the passenger door and I'll make it quick."

"I'm already wet. Let me help you."

His voice was deep and firm, and she found herself wanting to obey it. Too bad, she wasn't the obeying type.

"So am I, so a little more isn't going to make any difference. Let's do this."

She was wet and only going to get wetter when she left the relative safety and warmth of her car. She grabbed her purse and steeled herself, before opening the car door.

It was a deluge. She was soaked in an instant, her skin pelted by the pouring rain. She quickly pressed the door lock button for her car and pulled herself up and into the seat of the Land Rover, closing the door. She pushed her long, wet hair back from her face and tried to give her rescuer a thankful smile.

"Thanks. I was getting pretty worried driving in this. We have storms in Florida, but I'm familiar with the roads, and we have streetlights. I was afraid I was going to drive off the road with that wild wind."

The cab was dark, but she could see her rescuer give her a smile, too. He was a big man and seemed to take up a lot of space in the small interior. He radiated control and strength, even in the dark. Somehow, she knew he could handle the storm or anything else thrown at them. He also seemed to be soaked to the skin. She could smell his yummy masculine scent mixed with the scent of the rain. Did he look as good as he smelled?

"You're welcome. I would have been happy to help you into the car. Independent little cuss, aren't you?" She could hear his deep chuckle and blushed, glad it was dark and he couldn't see the telltale stain on her cheeks. She was independent, but she'd had to be. Starting her own jewelry design business at age twenty-one bred independence. She had learned to stand on her own two feet pretty quickly. She'd been told she was stubborn and impetuous, too. At least that was what her last few boyfriends had told her.

"And by the way, that's a Montana wind. You never would have made it to the house. The road is flooded out due to the storm. The Land Rover can make it through, but not your sedan. We'll get your car tomorrow. There's a towel on the seat behind you. It won't help much, but it's better than nothing."

His voice was warm and sexy, sliding over her already-heightened senses like a rich, mellow whiskey. Noelle felt the shiver of arousal zing up her spine in response. She pushed the feeling away and reached behind her and grabbed the towel gratefully. Now was not the time to be lusting after some cowboy in Montana, no matter how glad she was to not be driving anymore.

She was also shivering, cold, and wet, but determined not to complain. He had to be as uncomfortable as she was, but he wasn't whining. She might be independent and stubborn, but, dammit, she wasn't a whiner.

"I tried to call a few minutes ago, but I didn't have any bars on my cell phone."

"Cell phone coverage is spotty out here. We use radios around the ranch. I'll let them know we're on our way."

He picked up the handset.

"Hunter 5, this is Hunter 1."

"Hey, Hunter 1. Did you find Abby's big sister?"

He flicked a glance her way, before returning his eyes to the road.

"Sure did. And she's just like Abby described her. Stubborn as a mule. We'll be there in about half an hour."

She grimaced at Abby's description. Abby had always been the serene, biddable sister.

There was some static and then the voice continued.

"—can't make it back. Too many downed limbs, and the water is rising. Take Noelle to the cabin for the night. By tomorrow, the water will have receded."

Her rescuer was quiet for a minute before answering.

"Will do. Stay safe at the house."

He turned to her briefly. "We're heading to the cabin. We can't make it back, even in the Rover. You're not going to get hysterical on me, are you?"

Noelle bristled with indignation. "Of course not. You seem to have the situation under control. I'm not a woman given to hysterics, even if you didn't. I'd just take control of things."

His rich, deep laugh filled the cab of the SUV and made her heart speed up. He sounded sexy as hell. Did his looks match his voice?

"No need for that, Noelle. I'm completely in control. At all times."

He didn't say much as he navigated the roads. Noelle shuddered as she saw all the downed limbs and high water. There was no way her Honda would have made it this far. Now that she had time to look out the window, she wondered just how she had gotten as far as she had. He pulled off on a side road, and the headlights illuminated a small log house. Noelle could only hope the power wasn't out in this wind. She was dying for a hot shower or bath.

"Can you make a run for it? I'll go first and unlock the door, and you follow. As you said, we're already wet. We can get warm and dry when we're inside."

His voice was already making her warm. "You bet. I'll be right behind you."

She waited until he had opened the front door of the cabin, before running as fast as she could. She was dripping water by the time she stood in the dark, cool house. It was small, but clean and comfortable with a homey, country-style kitchen and living room combination.

"Um, does anyone live here?"

He started flicking on lights. "No one lives here. This is a cabin we use when we're working on the ranch and the weather turns on us. Like tonight."

So we're alone.

He turned to face her, and it was then she got her first good look. Her knees almost gave way. Dear Lord in heaven, even dripping wet, the man standing before her was gorgeous. He was dressed in a button-down Western-style shirt and faded jeans that molded a physique so perfect, Noelle could only stare. His face was tan and his jaw strong and square. His hair was dark and clung to his well-shaped head, but was curling at the ends. It made her want to plunge her hands into those locks and run her fingers through them. And those eyes…the clearest, lightest blue she had ever seen, almost the blue of a cloudless summer sky. She swallowed hard as she stared at the handsomest man she had ever seen. Her heart sped up, and she started to sweat, despite being chilled to the bone. She felt like she'd been hit by lightning.

Luckily, he was oblivious to her state. He gave her an encouraging smile and pointed to a small hallway off the living room. "There's a bathroom through there. Why don't you get a hot shower and I'll start some dinner. You must be hungry. It won't be anything fancy, but it will be hot."

He certainly was a polite rescuer, in addition to being God's gift to women.

"I'm starved, actually. And you must be cold, too."

"I'll get dry out here. I'll be fine. I'll find something for you to put on after your shower. I'm sure we have some shirts or something. They'll be too big, but dry."

She needed no further urging and retreated to the bathroom quickly, stripping off her wet clothes and stepping under the steaming, hot spray. Using the shampoo and soap, she scrubbed herself from top to bottom, luxuriating in the warmth. She wanted to linger, but her hunger won, and she stepped out, dried herself off, and reached for a stack of clothes he had left on the vanity. She was uncomfortably aroused for a moment thinking he had been in the room while she bathed, but the shower curtain was completely opaque. Was he similarly undressed on the other side of the door? She watched a drop of water slide down his wide chest and flat abs in her mind's eye. Her nipples peaked, and her pussy clenched at the erotic image.

Stop this, right now!

She pulled on the clothes and giggled at her reflection. The boxers were baggy, and the shirt was so long it almost reached her knees, but she was clean, warm, and dry for the first time in quite a while.

Way to impress the sexy, hot guy.

She combed the snarls out of her hair and made a face in the mirror. She looked like a drowned Irish Setter with her long, red hair. She was completely devoid of makeup, and her wardrobe left something to be desired, but it couldn't be helped. She wasn't here to have a romantic interlude with the hottest cowboy she had ever clapped eyes on. She was here to help her sister.

Keep reminding yourself of that.

* * * *

Cameron Hunter stood in the kitchen opening a can of beef stew and contemplating his lovely companion for the night when the subject of his thoughts joined him. She was wearing the shirt he had left and he couldn't stop the rush of lust that ran through him as she stood there looking shy, and sexy as all get-out. There was just something about a beautiful woman wearing a man's shirt. His shirt.

He had to steel himself not to throw her over his shoulder and head straight to the bedroom.

She was tiny, probably not much more than five feet tall. Her gorgeous, long red hair was tousled and starting to curl as it dried. It framed her heart-shaped face with its creamy skin, flushed cheeks, and the most unusual amber eyes he had ever seen. She was tugging on the hem of the shirt, obviously trying to cover as much of her shapely legs as she could. He grinned as he took in her mouthwatering curves and generous breasts. He hated stick-thin women, and this one would feel like heaven as he pressed her to the bed with his body.

She was also obviously stubborn as hell and didn't obey worth a damn. She'd been advised to stop for the night, and didn't. Then he'd told her he would help her out of the car, and she'd ignored him. She definitely needed her bottom warmed up and to be taught a lesson about listening to reason.

Despite her earlier bravado, she was looking pretty damn nervous. Her eyes were huge, and she was chewing on her bottom lip. His open perusal of her had made her uncomfortable, and he averted his gaze quickly. He was a Dom, for fuck's sake, and one look at this woman had his cock standing at attention and his breathing heavy. It hadn't been that long since he'd had a woman, had it? He took a few deep breaths to get control of his wayward hormones.

"I hope you like beef stew. I put some biscuits in the oven to go with it."

She gave him a shy smile, and he noticed how pink and full her lips were.

"Please let me help, um…You know my name, but I don't know yours."

Just being close to this woman was scrambling his brains. "Sorry, I forgot to introduce myself. I'm Cameron Hunter. Please, call me Cam."

"Hunter? You're related to Brody, Abby's fiancé? We're going to be family. That's great. Now how can I help? You've already gone above and beyond the call of duty tonight with rescuing me."

"After Abby told me you insisted on driving in the storm, I figured you'd need all the help you could get. I'm only sorry I didn't come for you earlier, but I only found out after dinner. If you want to help, you can set the table, if you like."

Cam nodded toward a cabinet, and Noelle pulled out bowls and flatware.

"We don't have any wine to help you warm up, but there are some beers in the refrigerator. So, do you like beef stew? You aren't one of those vegans, are you?"

She laughed, the sound almost musical. She seemed like a nice person, in addition to being one of the most beautiful women he had met in a very long time. Some women would have bitched and complained about getting wet, the food, the accommodations, but Noelle had been nothing but sweet and polite.

"Hardly. I'm a meat-and-potatoes girl, and a beer sounds great. Can I get you one, too?"

Cam nodded and stirred the beef stew, struggling to make conversation. He wasn't a talkative man by nature, so small talk didn't come easily to him. He wasn't shy. He just didn't say something unless he had something to say. He never understood those people who were always on their cell phones. Just what were they jabbering about all the time anyway? Noelle saved him from finding a topic.

"So is my sister driving you crazy with all this wedding stuff? Are she and Brody disgustingly in love and all kissy-kissy with each other? Don't be afraid to make her sleep in your barn. I assume you have a barn?"

Cam smiled. She was funny as well as beautiful and polite.

"A couple, actually. The wedding stuff hasn't been too bad. Brody isn't a kissy-kissy type, but Abby is very affectionate. He seems to enjoy it."

Cam had been a little envious that Brody had a woman who loved and cared about him that much. It had been a very long time since Cam had a special woman in his life. The older he got, the more he wanted to settle down with one woman he could make the center of his world. Someone who would submit in the bedroom and challenge him everywhere else.

"Well, I hope they like the rings I designed for them. A wedding ring is so personal, and they just told me to do anything I liked. It was kind of nerve-racking. I don't want them to be disappointed."

Noelle brushed past him as she set the bowls and silverware on the table. Her skin was warm, and her tantalizing scent teased his nostrils.

"I'm sure they'll love what you've done. I'd love to see it."

"They're locked away in my luggage. Speaking of luggage, will they be safe in my car all night? I suppose I'm asking a little late in the process. I was so happy to see you, I didn't even think to grab them."

"You had other things on your mind. They'll be fine. The road is private. No one should be on it unless they're headed to the ranch, and no one would be headed to the ranch on a night like this."

"Except me."

"Except you. But I can't say Abby didn't warn us about you. She said you're a full-speed-ahead type of person. *Fearless*, I believe is the word she used."

He turned off the stove and pulled open the oven. "I think this stew is heated up. The biscuits are ready to come out of the oven. I'm starved, and you must be, too. Let's get you fed and in bed."

He could have bitten off his tongue as he watched the heat flood Noelle's face. He tried to smooth it over and pretend he didn't notice.

"You must be exhausted. You can take the bedroom, and I'll sleep out here. The couch folds out."

Noelle shook her head. "You should take the bed. You rescued me, after all."

She didn't know him very well, but she would need to learn he didn't say or do things he didn't mean. He also found himself wanting to coddle and protect, and dominate this tiny woman. His Dom instincts were in overdrive—the protective, the disciplinary, and the sexual. There was something about this woman that brought them to the fore. He knew she wasn't normally this easygoing. Abby's tales of Noelle's stubbornness and her gorgeous red hair spoke of a woman who needed a strong man to love and care for her. He wondered if she had such a man in her life. He doubted it since she had no problem picking up her life and coming to Montana to help her sister.

He'd been alone a long time, and he was honest enough with himself to admit she was the first woman in years who interested him on more than just a sexual level. He wanted to get to know her better. A lot better. Luckily, she was staying for several weeks to help with the wedding. Was she submissive, too? Could he be that lucky?

"No, you'll take the bedroom. I'll be fine." She opened her mouth, but he held up his hand. "No arguments. I insist."

He used his best Dom voice, and she quickly acquiesced. *Interesting.*

"Well, thank you. You certainly are a gentleman. I'm not sure I remember spending time with a man as chivalrous as you are."

"Perhaps you're spending time with the wrong kind of men. Here in Montana, we take care of our women. Now let's eat and you can tell me all about you and Abby growing up."

Cam smiled inwardly. He had time to get to know this woman, and he was going to enjoy every single second of it. She didn't know it yet, but he was a man in pursuit of a beautiful woman. Something he hadn't been in a very long time.

* * * *

Noelle wriggled her toes in front of the roaring fire. She was toasty warm, full from dinner, and a little sleepy from the beer. They were relaxing in front of the fireplace. She had told Cam about her childhood, her book club friends, and her jewelry design business. Cam had told her he loved the outdoors, had thought about being a doctor instead of a rancher, and relaxed by watching sports and reading. He wasn't just gorgeous, he was smart and nice, too. An irresistible combination.

He was also, obviously, older than Brody. When his hair had dried, she had seen the strands of silver running through it, and his eyes had some crinkles around them when he smiled. She wondered how much older than Brody's twenty-five he was. He appeared to be about thirty-five or maybe forty. She knew some men went gray early. She was almost thirty herself and hadn't yet seen a gray hair, but it didn't mean they weren't around the corner.

She smiled in contentment as Cam shook his head at her statement. They were discussing politics, and so far they hadn't agreed on a thing. It was okay, though. They'd both agreed on their love for their careers and a preference for dogs over cats.

"People need to stand on their own two feet. Be independent. A society of dependence can never be truly free."

He took a sip from his beer and crossed his long legs in front of him. His shirt was unbuttoned halfway, and she could see the sprinkling of dark hair that covered his muscular chest. She wondered if it continued down those flat abs and to his cock. The bulge in his pants was impressive, and she found herself glancing at it way too often.

"I agree, Cam. But sometimes people need a hand up."

"A hand up, not a handout."

"How do you define a handout? If a mother and her children are homeless is it a handout or a hand up to give them food and shelter?"

"Why can't she get a job?"

"Because people who don't have addresses can't get jobs. Also, how is she going to find a job? She has no way to get cleaned up for an interview or get a phone call or e-mail from a prospective employer."

"She shouldn't have had kids she couldn't support."

"Okay, let's say she made bad choices. She didn't take proper precautions and had kids she couldn't support well. Then she lost her job and then her home. Maybe she got sick or one of her kids did. Should the kids suffer for her choices? Starve? Never be warm? You don't really believe that, do you?"

Cam's mouth twisted. "Of course not. Fuck, I'm not some heartless asshole. Listen, I'm not against homeless shelters or free clinics. I'm against a society that wants everything to be easy. Life isn't easy, for fuck's sake. It's hard damn work."

Noelle smiled at Cam's vehemence. "On this we can agree. I think people do want things to be easy. So many aren't willing to put in the hard work."

"Are you?"

She laughed at the question. If only he knew just how hard she'd had to work. "Yes. Believe me, I couldn't have built my business without a lot of hard work. I suspect you work pretty hard, too."

Cam nodded grimly. "Long, hard days. The SEALs have a saying, 'The only easy day was yesterday.' That's how it is on a ranch. Dirty, physical, sweaty work during the day and a pile of paperwork in the evenings."

"But you love it?"

Cam nodded. "I do. I thought about being a doctor for a while, but ranching is in my blood. It's my heritage. I look over the land and think about how generations of my family built this with grit and determination. It isn't easy. It's worth it."

She liked the way he respected the past. As an artist, she respected those who came before her. She liked his no-nonsense attitude and his passion for his work. She liked Cam Hunter way too much.

Cam held up his empty beer bottle with a smile.

"Another beer?"

Noelle shook her head. She was already sleepy enough. And maybe a little tipsy. Or perhaps it was the company of the handsomest man she'd ever met that made her light-headed?

Cam poked at the fire.

"You should head to bed. You look tuckered out."

Noelle yawned at the mere mention of sleep.

"I've had a big day. It's not every day I'm rescued from a storm and fed biscuits and beef stew by firelight."

Cam laughed and got to his feet, holding out his hand to help her.

"Never let it be said I don't know how to sweep a lady off her feet. The beer was imported."

She joined in the laughter and let him pull her to her feet. She hated for the evening to end. He was smart, funny, and charming. She could have talked to him for hours. A swift glance at the clock told her she practically had. It was well past midnight.

She stood close to him, his scent filling her nostrils and arousing senses that had lain dormant for quite a while. She hadn't met a man in a long time who affected her so strongly. In fact, she couldn't ever remember feeling this so quickly. A little voice in her head told her to play it cool and cautious, but it just wasn't in her nature.

"Well, good night. Thank you again for rescuing me and the dinner and the dry clothes."

Cam gave her a wry smile. "Such as they are. I'm glad I was able to rescue you. Get some sleep. You'll see Abby in the morning."

He pushed her long hair off her shoulder, and she froze as his fingers brushed her cheek, sending a streak of pleasure straight to her pussy. The skin burned where his fingers had touched her. He dropped his hand quickly.

She started heading for the bedroom. She needed some space between them. Suddenly, the air had been filled with...desire and anticipation. She liked to grab at life, but she wasn't going to sleep with this man only hours after meeting him. That wasn't in her nature either.

She paused at the hallway to glance back at him. His expression was intense, his features grim. He felt it, too.

"Good night, Cam. See you in the morning."

She climbed into bed, but it was a long time until she slept. *Just when you least expect your life to take a turn, it does.*

Her thoughts were filled with the man in the next room. Her time in Montana would be interesting, no doubt. She just needed to try and not lose her head. Or her panties.

Chapter Two

The sun was shining, and Noelle craned her neck to get a better look at the massive ranch house up ahead, as they drove up the long driveway. She was sorry her time with Cam was coming to an end.

She was also very attracted to him. Very. By the time she had headed off to bed last night, her whole body had ached with desire. She wondered if he had felt the same pull toward her as she did him. She would never have slept with him last night, but her body had put up a good fight. Several times she had woken and thought about joining him on the fold-out couch.

"Abby's going to be real happy to see you. You'll get to meet most of the family, too. Don't let them overwhelm you. If they start making you crazy, you just come to me. I'll protect you."

Noelle smiled. She knew Cam was only joking, but she liked his protective manner. In any other man, it would have been annoying, but with this man, it fit.

"I'm sure they'll be fine. Was Abby overwhelmed?"

She and her sister didn't come from a large family.

"No, but she had Brody there to run interference."

The Land Rover pulled up to the front of the house, and Noelle pushed the car door open as a stream of people rushed out of the front door. Noelle immediately recognized Abby running straight for her. She held out her arms for her baby sister.

"Abby, I made it!"

Abby grabbed and hugged her tightly. No one would know they were sisters by looking at them. Abby was tall, willowy, and blonde. The only thing they had in common was the unusual color of their eyes. Not quite brown, not quite gold, they had inherited their mother's amber eyes. It was those amber eyes that were bright with unshed tears.

"Elle, I'm so glad you're here! I was so worried about you and Cam in the storm."

Noelle hugged her sister one more time before giving her a wry smile.

"I know, and I'm sorry. Thank you for sending him, by the way. I'd probably be coyote chow by now if you hadn't."

"No way we'd let you get eaten by coyotes, Noelle. Can I call you Noelle? I'm Brody Hunter, your soon-to-be brother-in-law."

An extremely handsome young man held out his hand with a big smile. He had brown hair, blue eyes, and dimples. Abby was a lucky woman. He was a real cutie, and looked a lot like Cam. She shook his hand with a smile.

"Yes, please call me Noelle. It's very nice to meet you finally. I've heard so much about you. About you and your family."

The family appeared to be lined up on the steps of the wraparound porch. The two handsome men giving her flirtatious smiles looked just enough like Brody to be his brothers. There was also an older woman and an older man with silver just touching the wings of his closely cropped hair. Both man and woman were handsome and had welcoming smiles on their faces. Brody waved to the young men first.

"These are my twin older brothers, Caden and Lucas. That's my Uncle Colt and his wife, Julie. They live in the house just a couple of miles from here on the ranch. They've got three sons and a daughter, but they weren't able to greet you this morning."

Noelle began shaking hands but wondered if Cam wasn't a brother, was he a cousin of some sort?

"And of course, you've met my dad, Cameron Hunter. We hope you enjoy your stay here, Noelle."

The air sucked from her lungs, and the world tilted sideways. Cam Hunter was Brody's dad.

Outstanding. I want to fuck the brains out of Abby's future father-in-law.

* * * *

Cam held the mug of steaming coffee between his hands and stared unseeingly at the back pasture. After Noelle had been introduced to his family, he had taken her suitcases to her room and headed out here to the barn to lick his wounds.

"Hidin' out here, Cam?"

Cam's brother, Colt, was heading right for him. No way could he avoid this conversation. He fought his irritation at the interruption and set the coffee down with a sigh. Except for his bedroom and man cave, which everyone knew was sacred, he was never really alone here at the ranch. It didn't bother him most of the time, but right now he could do without his brother's company.

"Or are you pouting?"

Cam gave his brother a scathing look. "Pouting? Are you fucking kidding me? Why would I be pouting?"

Colt chuckled and went to pour himself a cup of coffee from the coffeemaker they kept running all day long in the barn. Ranching was a twenty-four-hour-a-day business.

"Because that pretty little filly abandoned you and headed to spend time with her sister instead. She's a looker, Cam. You always did have good taste."

"I hardly see how my taste in women comes into this, Colt. If she had been a dog, I wouldn't have left her to freeze and starve in her car last night."

Colt sat down on a bale of hay and stretched out his long legs with a chuckle, sipping his coffee. "No, but you wouldn't have been so territorial this morning when you brought her home. You damn near peed on her in front of your sons to mark your ownership."

Cam was not amused. His brother could be a real asshole

sometimes.

"I was not territorial. She doesn't belong to me."

Colt laughed. "Yet. You had your arm around her like she was a prize and a furious scowl for Caden and Lucas when they were giving her the eye. You want her. Admit it. You want to put a collar around her neck. Damn, big brother, it's about time."

Cam opened his mouth to argue, but snapped it shut. His asshole of a brother was right. He did want Noelle. Badly. One night and morning with her hadn't been nearly enough. She was smart, funny, sexy, and Cam wanted to explore the simmering heat he knew he hadn't imagined between the two of them. She might be the woman he had been waiting for. A woman he could love.

Cam sat down on the hay bale next to Colt and sighed. He really hated when his brother had that smug, satisfied look on his face.

"Yes, I do want her. She's the kind of woman I've wanted to meet. I thought I was doing my duty going out to help her last night. I never expected to enjoy the time with her. I thought I would just have to deal with it. But, she's amazing. She's not only beautiful. She's the whole package. I thought she was attracted to me, too, until this morning. Did you see her face when she found out I was Brody's dad? Dear God, she looked at me like I had one foot in the grave and another on a banana peel. It never for a minute occurred to me our age difference might be a problem. Shit, I'm only forty-nine. That's not old. Didn't Abby say Noelle was going to be thirty in a few weeks?"

Colt barked in laughter. "She did say that. And Noelle didn't look at you in horror over your age. She just looked surprised. I'm guessing she thought you were Brody's older brother, not his father. You should feel complimented." Colt slapped Cam on the back. "And when you say she's the whole package, does that mean she's submissive, too, you lucky son of a bitch?"

Cam stood up and started pacing the hay-strewn floor. "I don't know. I get a vibe from her that she likes it when I take control and get protective. I also get a vibe that she's never submitted to anyone or anything her entire life. Her submission won't be easily won. She doesn't like to obey from what I've experienced." He stopped in front of his brother. "Do you really think she wasn't turned off by my age? She looked gob-smacked by the news."

"Shit, yes, she was surprised, but you could feel the sexual tension between you two. It was thick and it didn't dissipate when she found out you're as old as Methuselah. As for her submission, no submission worth winning comes easily. You know as well as I do."

Colt certainly did know it. Julie had led his brother on a merry chase almost thirty years ago before she had agreed to wear his collar. They were proof a lifelong Dominant-submissive relationship was not only possible, but could bring both parties happiness and fulfillment. Cam had always wanted what Colt had with Julie. His own marriage had crashed and burned fifteen years ago. He had learned a great deal from his marriage and divorce, and one of those things was that good women were hard to find. This woman had literally driven herself to his remote ranch. He wasn't going to let this chance pass him by.

Cam nodded, determined now his mind was made up. He smiled as he imagined her restrained at the club to the St. Andrew's Cross. She would be a sight to behold with all that fiery red hair and amber eyes. How long would it take for her to beg him to let her come? Would she struggle against his domination, and then finally, sweetly surrender? He hoped so.

"You're right, Colt. No woman or submission is worth anything if you don't have to work to win. Do you think I'm too old to woo the beautiful Noelle?"

Colt snorted with laughter. "Probably. But, I doubt you'll let that stop you. Just a word of warning, though."

Cam frowned. "Warning? Are you warning me she may not be submissive? I won't force her, Colt. This has to be what she wants, too. I won't take. I'll only accept what she willingly gives me."

Colt shook his head. "I know that. You're a good Dom. One of the best. My warning is about Gwen. She'll be visiting for the wedding, and she'll cause trouble if she thinks you're happy. Watch out for her meddling. You and I both know that woman is a royal bitch."

Cam knew quite well. Gwen was his ex-wife and worked to make his life difficult on a regular basis despite being divorced for over a decade.

"Point taken. I'll keep an eye on Gwen. You, too. I can't be everywhere at once. I don't want Gwen pulling any shit with Noelle. She wouldn't stand a chance with Gwen."

Cam turned to head back to the main house, Colt's warning ringing in his ears. He was going to take his chance with Noelle, and he wasn't going to let Gwen anywhere near her.

* * * *

"I can't wait to see it!"

Abby pushed Noelle into her bedroom and jumped on the bed. Noelle shook her head, laughing, and opened her suitcase. Cam must have brought them up while Abby was showing her around the ranch. He was so caring and always a gentleman.

"I hope you like the ring set. If you don't, I don't know what I'll do. You'll have to make do with them, until I can redo them."

Noelle was nervous. She loved the way the wedding set had turned out, but Abby and Brody were the ultimate judges. She needed to show Abby the rings and find out if she hated them or not. She pulled the velvet boxes from her bag and handed them to her sister.

"Since you said Brody won't wear his ring every day due to the hazards of working on the ranch, I decided to put stones in his wedding band. Go ahead. Open it. I can't stand not knowing if you like them or not."

Abby fumbled with the box but managed to open it. She was quiet as she stared at the rings that Noelle had designed for her. The silence stretched on as Abby continued to stare down at the rings.

God, she must hate it.

"If you don't like it, I can do something else."

Abby looked up at Noelle, her eyes bright with tears.

"I love it. I simply love it. I can't believe how beautiful it is. I wish Brody weren't working outside right now because I want him to see this. You're a genius, sis."

Noelle felt her body go slack with relief. She didn't realize how tense she had been holding herself until this moment.

"Look at Brody's ring, too. Do you think he'll like it?"

Abby snapped open the second box and gave her a brilliant smile.

"He'll love it. It's manly, but not clunky and big. It's perfect. All the rings are perfect. Do you think it would be bad luck to try them on?"

Noelle smiled in relief. Abby really liked the rings. "No, I don't think it will be bad luck at all."

She helped Abby slip first the delicate yellow gold wedding band on her finger. Abby was a horticulturist and Noelle had designed delicate vines and flowers twining around the band with tiny diamonds and sapphires. Diamonds were Brody's birthstone and sapphires were Abby's. Then the engagement ring slid on her finger with one ornate vine studded with diamonds circling the large, round center diamond. It was delicate and old-fashioned, just like Abby.

"It looks beautiful on you, Ab. Does it fit?"

Abby was grinning now. "Perfectly. Now I don't want to take them off. Perhaps I can convince Brody to get married today."

Brody's wedding band was a wide gold band with the twining vines and a channel of diamonds. It was simple, but the lines were strong.

"If anyone can convince Brody to move up the wedding it's you. I'm glad you chose yellow gold. It will go with so much of your other jewelry. That necklace you have on is very pretty."

Abby blushed as her hand flew up to the necklace, fingering the heavy links.

"It's a gift from Brody. I never take it off, except to wear a more formal one. It's…it's my collar, Noelle."

Noelle replayed the words in her head a few times before responding.

"Your collar? I can see it's a choker-style necklace, if that's what you mean."

Abby shook her head and chewed her bottom lip. Noelle could see her sister struggling with something.

"Spit it out, Abby. You're dying to. I can see that."

"It's my collar, Elle. I'm Brody's submissive, and he is my Dominant. All the Hunter family lives like this. I knew I needed to tell you in case you saw something while you're here that you didn't understand."

Noelle forced herself to stay quiet while she gathered her thoughts. She knew about these kinds of relationships from her book club reading, of course. She had always been fascinated by the exchange of power and how intimate the couples seemed to be. The level of trust in the relationships was off the charts compared to many vanilla relationships. But an entire family of Dominant-submissive relationships?

Wait, is Cam a Dominant or a submissive?

A Dominant. No question. His air of calm control, and protectiveness screamed Dominant. She waited for the wave of disappointment, but it never came. She had never thought of herself as submissive and always assumed she would want a submissive man. But the thought of a man kneeling at her feet and obeying her commands suddenly seemed very wrong. In fact, she was having a hard time even picturing it.

"Noelle, say something. You're expression is negative."

She was shaking her head at the images of a man on his knees, submitting. Instead she was substituting images of herself kneeling at Cam's feet. The erotic thought made her nipples peak and cream drip from her pussy. She was shocked at her body's response. Maybe she was a little bit submissive, after all. Or maybe just with this dominant man.

"It's okay, Abby. I'm not going to judge you. Honestly. I've read about this stuff, you know. I'm not naive. Does he treat you well? Are you happy?"

Abby laughed and lay back on the pillows with a dreamy smile. "He treats me like a princess and yes, I'm very happy. He doesn't tell me what to eat or what to wear, but he looks after my welfare, and I know I am the most important thing in his life."

Noelle felt a twinge of envy. She had never been the most important thing in anyone's life.

"I'm happy for you then. I really am. So, the whole family is like this?"

Noelle tried to sound casual.

Abby rolled over on her stomach and admired her new rings. "Yes. I guess they have been for generations. Brody and his brothers are all Dominants, plus his uncle, oh, and his father, of course. Do you think Brody will look like Cam in twenty-five years?"

Noelle was still trying to process the fact that Cam was a Dominant.

"Probably. He looks very much like him now."

Abby gave her a sly smile. "Maybe I'll fix you up with Lucas or Caden. I know you've always said you like being in charge in relationships, but I think that's a bunch of bull. I think you'd like a dominant man. There's nothing like an alpha male in bed." Abby giggled and looked around to see if anyone was around. "I've never come as hard or as often as I do with Brody. He's an awesome lover. I bet his brothers are, too."

How about his father?

Noelle shook her head, but wouldn't meet Abby's eyes. "I'm not interested in Lucas or Caden. I'm sure they're nice, but I'm only going to be here a short time. I don't think getting involved would be a good idea."

Abby tugged off her rings and placed them carefully in the

jewelry boxes.

"The Hunter men have a way of sneaking under your radar. You never know, Elle. You just may have met your match in these men."

Noelle had a suspicion Abby was right. One Hunter man in particular was very dangerous to her heart.

* * * *

The wind whipped through her hair and chilled her cheeks, exhilaration running through her veins. Cam, Abby, and Brody had insisted she get a tour of the ranch. Not on horseback, as she had expected, but on the back of an ATV. Noelle laughed as Cam hit a small hill at full speed sending them sailing in the air for a few feet before landing back down with a jolt. Her bones were rattled, but she didn't care. This was the most fun she'd had in forever. Cam was driving the ATV like a bat out of hell, but she felt safe as a lamb with him. Every movement of the vehicle was carefully calculated and controlled, just like its driver.

She was pressed close to his solid, muscular back, her arms wrapped tightly around his lean middle. His masculine scent mixed with the outdoors and she pressed closer, breathing him in. He felt strong and warm, and she couldn't stop her fingers flexing on his rock-hard abs. Even through his jacket she could feel that there wasn't an ounce of spare flesh on him. He was all muscle.

He stopped under some oak trees and pointed to a vast field in the distance. "That's a hay field. Hay is a cash crop. We grow more hay than we need for the cattle and we sell the rest."

"You sell it? Can you really make money on it?"

Brody and Abby came up behind them on another ATV and stopped next to them.

"Damn, Dad, I can't keep up with you. How did you get so far in front of us?"

Cam laughed. "I still know a few tricks I haven't taught you.

Noelle and I were talking about growing hay for profit."

Brody grimaced. "Haying is back-breaking work."

Cam nodded toward the field. "But profitable. Now that you're going to be a married man, I think you need a part of this ranch to run yourself. Something you can lead and be proud of. I was thinking you might want to take control of the haying operations."

Brody's face broke into a grin. "You mean it, Dad?"

"Wouldn't offer if I didn't mean it. What do you say?"

"I say I'm the man for the job. Don't worry, Dad, I'll work hard and make sure everything runs like clockwork."

"I have all the confidence you will, Brody. I don't know about you all, but I'm starving. Let's take a break and have some lunch."

Cam helped Noelle off the ATV as Abby rushed toward them, her face glowing. "Thank you, Cam. Brody won't let you down. I'll help him with the paperwork stuff so he can concentrate on the operations."

"You and Brody make a good team. My son is a lucky man."

Abby blushed and bustled off to help Brody set up lunch. They had leather bags with a couple of blankets and a picnic. Noelle's stomach growled. The fresh air had peaked her appetite. Cam chuckled. "I think you're hungry, too. Let's get something in your stomach. You need to keep your energy up on a ranch."

Noelle crossed her arms over her chest and gave Cam a smile. "Did you have this planned the whole time? Bring Brody and Abby out here and then tell him the news? They're so excited."

"Not the whole time. But it seemed as good a time as any when I realized how close we were to this hay field. Brody and Abby will do a fine job. I can put my energies elsewhere. There's always work to do on a ranch."

Noelle arched an eyebrow. "But you're here with me today, showing me around the place. Don't you have work to do?"

"Yes."

Noelle blinked. "Yes? That's it?"

His blue eyes twinkled. "How about, yes, I have work to do and yes, I'm here with you. As I said, there's always work to do on a ranch. The work isn't going anywhere, but you won't be here forever. If I want to get to know you, then I have to make time to spend with you."

Noelle felt her heart speed up. "You want to get to know me?"

Cam gave her a gentle smile. "I do. Is that okay with you?"

"Um, sure. Yeah. But...why?"

Cam reached for her hands and gave them a squeeze. "Because I like you. I enjoyed spending time with you last night. I think you enjoyed it, too. Am I wrong?"

Noelle couldn't deny the truth of his words. "No, I had fun last night if you don't count the almost perishing in a storm part."

"You never came close to perishing. I would never have let anything like that happen."

Noelle looked up at him through her lashes, feeling the heat of his hands. "Where do we go from here?"

Cam put his arm around her shoulders and headed toward the picnic Brody and Abby were setting out. "We eat. Then we finish touring the ranch. Maybe later we can spend more time together. I'll let you try and convince me that smaller defense spending is a good idea."

Noelle laughed. "Coupled with real tax reform it could lower our deficit."

"You sure know how to sweet-talk a man. Let's eat."

Noelle let Cam lead her over to the blankets, but she wasn't paying any attention to the food. Her focus was on the handsomest man she had ever met. A man who was not only sexy but nice as well. She wanted to get to know him, too. This was the start of something. She could feel it.

* * * *

Noelle wrapped her arms around herself as a cold breeze raised goose bumps on her skin. The day had been pleasantly warm with only a chilly breeze in the morning. According to Abby, however, the nights still got quite cold. She could be toasty next to the fireplace inside, but had felt the need to get away from all the people in the house. It wasn't unpleasant, just different. Many evenings found her eating takeout, alone in her condo, while she worked. Tonight there had been eleven people at the massive dining table. Cam had sat at the head, clearly the leader of this loving and lively family. She jumped in surprise when she felt something warm wrap around her.

Cam, with a blanket.

She'd know his scent anywhere. He smelled of the outdoors and something that was so intrinsically Cam. Her heart started beating faster when he didn't move back immediately. He stayed close behind her, and she could feel the heat come off his body and feel his warm breath on her neck and shoulders. She wanted to turn around and press herself against his muscled hardness. She swallowed the sudden lump in her throat.

"Thank you. I guess I was getting chilly. I just came out for some air."

She felt rather than heard Cam's chuckle.

"And to freeze to death? Your Florida blood is probably a little thin to be standing out here in just a sweater. Did the family drive you out here?"

"No. Well, kind of. I'm just not used to being around this many people. My job is rather solitary. I spend much of my time alone. You must be used to this, though."

His large hands ran up and down her arms, sending her arousal into orbit. Her panties were getting quite damp, and her breasts were straining against her lace bra. She didn't remember ever wanting a man this badly. She wanted to feel his hands on her quivering body.

"I guess so, but I like to come out here and have some quiet time, too. Do you want to go for a walk? I promise we'll stay dry."

She was far from dry. Honey was dripping from her pussy, and her nipples were hard and tight. She couldn't help but react to all his maleness so close to her. The fact that he was a Dom was only adding fuel to the fire. She had been fantasizing about being with him all day.

She'd had an entire day to think about the fact he was Brody's dad. She was sure he was older than she was, but he didn't seem too perturbed by the fact she was younger. Age was just a number, anyway. She was attracted to this man more than any man she had ever met. She wasn't going to let a silly thing like age get in the way.

Nor was she going to let the brevity of her stay here in Montana interfere. No relationship promised a forever after. Perhaps a few weeks were all she and Cam would have together. It would have to be enough.

His arm around her shoulders pulled her close to the warmth of his body as they walked toward the barn. She breathed in his heady scent and pressed herself closer. She barely came up to his shoulder. He made her feel very small and petite, yet safe at the same time. He was a man who could take care of her. That was clear. Not that she needed anyone to take care of her. She had been taking care of herself for years and doing a good job of it. But tonight, for a few minutes, she was content to lean on Cam's strength and let him make her feel warm and safe.

He stopped outside the barn and turned her toward him. The moon was full and it cast a light over his handsome features. His expression was intense and passionate.

"We need to get something straight, Noelle. Here and now."

Before she could reply, his head swooped down, and his lips captured hers. His tongue ran along the seam of her lips and she opened them willingly, eagerly to his seeking tongue. It explored her mouth as if he owned it, rubbing her tongue with his, before tickling the roof of her mouth. She was dizzy with want, and she clung to his wide shoulders, her world narrowing to just the two of them. She moved closer and felt his hard cock press into her soft belly. His size was impressive, and her fingers itched to caress him. Her hands trailed down his chest and his flat stomach before his hands caught hers.

"Not yet, precious. First of all, we need to talk. Second, you need permission before you touch me. That's one of my rules."

His voice was deep and firm, and she felt her pussy flood with moisture in response to his dominant tone.

So much for being a Domme.

He put a little space between them, but still held her in the circle of his arms.

"I'm forty-nine years old, precious. You need to know that, and you need to decide if that's okay. I've been divorced for fifteen years with three sons who I brought up without much help from my nightmare of an ex-wife. She lives to make my life miserable. I know you're twenty-nine, and we're about to become in-laws. If we get involved, I won't hide this from everyone. We won't sneak around or pretend we're just friends. Everyone will know how I feel."

She looked up into his beautiful blue eyes.

"How do you feel?"

He smiled and trailed a finger down her cheek, leaving her skin tingling wherever he touched.

"I feel lucky. Incredibly lucky to have met someone like you at this point in my life. I'd pretty much given up on meeting someone I could possibly be serious about. Is that too direct? I'm not saying I'm in love. Not yet. But if we did fall in love, I sure wouldn't be unhappy about it."

Noelle admired his strong, no-nonsense attitude.

"Your age doesn't bother me. Yes, I was surprised you were Brody's dad. I will admit that. But the twenty years seems meaningless when we're together. I wouldn't be unhappy if we fell in love either. I know I'm younger, but I was starting to give up, too. It seemed like every guy I dated had something really wrong with him."

Cam laughed and pulled her closer. She luxuriated in being this close to him and pressed her face into his chest. She could feel his heartbeat and the rise and fall of his chest.

"When you get to know me, you might decide there's something wrong with me, too."

He pulled away, and she started to protest, but his finger on her lips silenced her.

"Abby told Brody that she told you our little family secret. Except that this family secret is pretty well known around here. We need to talk about this. I need to know what's going on under all that fiery, red hair."

She chose her words carefully. "I was surprised, of course. A family of Doms isn't too common, I would imagine."

"You might be surprised about that, precious. And we're not always Doms. If someone in our family is a sub, that's just fine. This is how we live our life, that's all."

Noelle frowned. "You mean there are lots of families out there who—never mind. That's not important. Yes, Abby told me and I was pretty surprised. I've read about this sort of thing. I have quite a collection of erotic romance books. It's always fascinated me, honestly."

Noelle cursed her red hair and fair skin as she felt heat rising in her cheeks. She didn't know why she had told him about her reading material.

"Ah yes, the book club you're in. I think I know the answer, but I'll ask anyway. Have you ever submitted to a man?"

Noelle shook her head. "No. In fact, until I met you, I thought I was dominant."

His hands ran down her back, soothing and caressing, and sending liquid heat to her cunt.

"I'm not surprised. You were fascinated by the power exchange and the dynamics, but hadn't met anyone you could imagine trusting enough to submit. So you fantasized about being dominant. It makes perfect sense to me. There's a saying that the best submissives were once Dominants."

"I've never heard that saying, but I can see now why it might be true. The trust one has to have always seemed like something I could never fathom."

"And now?"

She buried her face into his chest again. It was hard to look him in the eye and admit these things.

"I've been thinking about it all day, Cam. I tried to imagine dominating you, but it was all wrong. All I could think about was playing out some of the scenes I've read about. I've been aroused all day."

Cam's arms tightened and lifted her until she was looking him straight in the eyes.

"Uh-uh, don't hide your face. I want to see you when you say that. I want you to know that I've been aroused all day, too. Hell, I was aroused last night. I want you to think about this tonight. I'm a Dom, Noelle. I was born this way, and I will die this way. I will demand your submission and push your limits. I will accept nothing less than all of you. I will also cherish, care, and protect you with everything that I am. You will get all of me, too. This isn't play to me. This is how I live my life. If you think you can handle this kind of trust and honesty, I'd like to pursue a relationship with you."

Noelle started to answer but his hand came up to halt her words.

"I know you live in Florida and hell, we just met. But this thing between us is strong. I'd like to explore it while you're here. That's what I'm asking you. I'm not asking for forever. Not yet. I'm just asking for a chance to show you what this lifestyle means. Sort of a try before you buy."

Noelle started to speak, but he pressed his fingers to her lips.

"I want you to think about this, precious girl. Think very hard and long. This is a commitment between us. At least a commitment while you're here in Montana. I don't want a tourist. I want someone who is open to exploring something out of her comfort zone. I want you to explore it with me. No half-in or half-out."

Noelle crossed her arms over her chest and gave him a saucy smile. He didn't know her very well if he thought she did anything halfway.

"I'll think about it. I don't commit to anything unless I'm really sure. When I do commit, I'm in it to win it."

"I figured that about you. I also know you have very little fear, Noelle. You need to be damn sure you want to give this a try. Let's head back to the house then. If you decide your answer is yes, then at dinner tomorrow night, you sit at my right hand at the dinner table. That's where my woman and sub should be. If you choose no, sit anywhere else. No hard feelings. I know what I'm asking is a lot. I'll understand if you decide against this. I'll be disappointed, but I'll understand."

They walked quietly back to the house, and he hesitated at the door.

"Go on in. I'm going to stay out here awhile."

He kissed her lips softly. "Dream of me, Noelle."

She knew she would.

Chapter Three

"Hands behind your back, my slave. Only your mouth."

He waited while she positioned herself correctly, then leaned forward on her knees to engulf the head of his hard cock into the warm cavern of her mouth. He hissed in pleasure, but kept his face impassive. It wouldn't do to let his slave know how affected he was by her ministrations. Better to keep her guessing.

"Swallow me all down, slave. All of me. You should be able to pleasure my balls with your tongue when my cock is down your throat. That's how a proper blow job is given. I'll not accept anything but your best."

His slave took a deep breath and loosened her jaw to allow his cock to slip farther into her mouth and nudge the back of her throat. She choked for a moment, but he remained where he was, letting her fight her gag reflex. She would need to learn to control it.

"Breathe through your nose, slave."

He tangled his fingers in her long, dark hair and tugged at her head, urging her to take him deeper. She was obviously reluctant, but he waited patiently while she worked to relax, taking him deeper with each stroke of her mouth and tongue. He arched his hips and pressed his cock deep into her throat. Her hands came up in fear, then relaxed behind her again when she realized she wasn't choking.

"Swallow on me, slave."

She followed his instructions, and he bit back his groan as his balls pulled tight to his body. He fucking loved it when a sub on her knees sucked his cock. This sub especially had a talented tongue. Her reticence to take every inch he had to give her would give him an excuse to punish her afterward. He would enjoy turning her ass a bright red, and then fucking it.

He anchored his hands on each side of her head, holding his cock as far as she could take him.

"I'm coming, slave. Swallow every drop."

He let go of his tight control and felt the pleasure run through his body. His cock jerked with each spurt of cum he shot deep into her throat. He watched as she frantically tried to swallow every bit of the hot load, and he smiled as he finally pulled back, leaving the head of his cock in her warm, wet mouth.

"Lick me clean, slave."

"Holy hell, that is hot." Brianne Hart fanned herself and rolled her eyes. Noelle was attending the book club meeting via Skype. Cam had very nicely offered her his office, and she was currently perched at his desk with the door locked. She wasn't sure she was ready for the entire household to know about her reading proclivities. Lisa Hart and Sara Jameson were there with Brianne, but Tori was absent due to a business trip to New York. She was currently on a flight headed for JFK Airport.

Noelle had been attending the book club weekly for several years now. She was as close to these women as her own sister. Lisa Hart was the glamorous one. Blonde and beautiful, she was the wife of a successful attorney. She also had a raunchy sense of humor and a down-to-earth personality that meant she never took herself too seriously. Brianne Hart was auburn-haired, funny, and vivacious. She had a young son, Kade, from her first marriage and a baby girl, Paige, from her marriage to Nate Hart, Lisa's brother-in-law. Brianne was their artistic genius and mother earth.

Sara Jameson was quiet and dignified. Her long, dark hair and pixie-like features often fooled people into thinking she was naive and weak. She was actually a strong woman who had been through her husband's death and had been raising her toddler son alone when she had fallen in love with not one, but two men. Jeremy, her husband's brother, and his partner Cole were now the men in Sara's life, and they adored her unashamedly. Last, but certainly not least, there was Tori Cordell. Dark-haired and sophisticated, she was creative and brilliant. She wrote children's books for a living but was so intelligent she could have been a nuclear scientist. She was raising her teenage sons alone since her husband had died after a long illness.

Sara made a face. "He's a little impersonal for me. I like a Dom who gives a shit about his sub. This guy is iffy so far. He keeps her safe and gives her pleasure, but he seems a little removed from it all."

Brianne plucked a chocolate from the gold box on the table. "Maybe he has intimacy issues."

Lisa arched a perfectly shaped eyebrow. "Then he shouldn't be a Dom, should he? Noelle, what do you think of this guy?"

Noelle took a deep breath. These were her best friends in the whole world and today of all days, she needed them.

"I think you're right. He seems a little cold to me. But, actually, that's not what I want to talk about today. I want to talk to all of you about something personal."

Brianne closed the cover on her e-reader. "We're listening. How personal?"

Noelle leaned closer to the camera. "Very personal. I really need your advice. I'm actually kind of glad Tori's on an airplane. I wanted to talk to you. I wanted to talk about what it's like to be a submissive."

Brianne, Sara, and Lisa glanced at each other, and Lisa sat back in her chair casually crossing one leg over the other.

"Why would you ask us about that? Why would we know anything except what we read?"

Noelle shook her head. "Don't pull that shit with me. I've seen you with your husbands when you think no one is looking. I've heard you, both of you, call them Master when you think no one can hear. I've seen Sara's men spank her when they think no one is watching. I need your help here, not your stonewalling. I've met a Dom, for fuck's sake. A Dom who could just be the man of my dreams. He wants to get to know me, and I want to get to know him. I need to know what I'm getting into. You've been my friends for years. This is no time to pretend!"

Noelle's voice had gone up an octave and sounded a little desperate by the end of her little speech. Lisa, Sara, and Brianne visibly relaxed. Brianne even laughed.

"Well, I guess the cat is officially out of the bag, then? How long have you known?"

Noelle smiled. "A while. I suspected Lisa and Conor years ago, then you and Nate got together...Well, it seemed like you guys weren't trying to hide it, honestly. I'm not 100 percent about Sara, but enough to bring this up in front of her."

Lisa fiddled with her cocktail glass. "Perhaps. I'm not fond of keeping secrets from my close friends. Well, you've met a Dom, huh? Who would have ever thought? He must be quite a man to get you to think about submitting. Tell us every detail and don't leave anything out."

"Maybe I was in denial about being submissive. I don't know. I just know when I'm with him I have to fight the urge to fall to his feet. Did I mention he's incredibly hot, too? There's just something about him that makes me feel desired and safe. He's nice, and smart, and we don't agree on a damn thing having to do with politics. Oh shit. And he's Brody's dad. I forgot to tell you that."

Lisa choked on her cosmo. "Brody's dad? Isn't Brody your future brother-in-law? How old is this Dom, anyway?"

"Forty-nine and every inch gorgeous. He's in amazing shape. He looks forty, tops."

Sara took the glass from Lisa's hand and set it on the table. "If you want to fall at his feet, he must be one hell of a Dom. He must have an alpha vibe to die for. So what's the problem? You seem okay with your submissive side. Or is that the issue?"

"He asked me to commit to exploring this side of myself while I was in Montana. No declarations of love and commitment past these weeks until the wedding. It's just happened so fucking fast. I met him and here I am contemplating a relationship with him."

Brianne propped her chin in her hands as she leaned on the table. "It's nice if you have the luxury of knowing someone for years like I did Nate. We already had trust. I just had to relax and let the love grow."

Lisa smiled. "I suppose that would be nice. Taking your time and all. But I fell for Conor the minute I met him. Bam! It hit me like a ton of bricks. I looked at him and knew this was the man I was meant to be with forever. And we were really just college kids. You and this man are adults. You know what you want and don't want by now. You don't need a lot of time. You just need the right man. Sounds like you have one hell of a candidate up there."

Noelle thought about how much she had enjoyed the time they had spent together. "He is. He's...a man among men, if you know what I mean."

Sara whistled. "Oooo, I like the sound of that. Besides, you're not the type to waste any time. You go after what you want. Go after him."

Noelle shook her head. "I think he'll want to be in charge of going after things. He seems to like control."

Brianne sipped her drink. "So do you, Elle. Are you okay submitting to him?"

"I want to try, Bri. The idea excites me. Hell, he excites me. He's not asking for a lifetime. He's asking me to give this a trial run. If I hate it, can't I say a safe word or something?"

Lisa laughed. "Yes, you can safe word, although I hope it doesn't get to that point, Elle. Just talk to him. Tell him what you want, what you fear. Let him know if you have any hard limits. If he's a good Dom, he'll respect them and you."

"He will respect me. I can tell that about him already. I know I'm moving fast and taking a big chance, but what I feel is so strong. He seems worth taking a leap of faith for."

She could see how Brody respected Abby and Colt respected Julie. She knew Cam would respect her if she submitted to him.

"I know I've said that couldn't ever imagine submitting. And I couldn't. Not before this man. I don't think I could even picture submitting to anyone else. What I need from you guys is some, well, training. I don't want to disappoint him. Can you help me? Teach me some of the rules?"

Sara held up her hands. "We just play at it. We're not serious. I'll defer to Lisa and Brianne."

Lisa grinned. "We'd be happy to. However, you should know, every Dom has their own rules. Their own way of doing things. We may teach you something he doesn't like or want you to do. But, I think he will be thrilled that you tried to learn some things for him. That would melt Conor's heart in an instant. Doms, good Doms, have soft hearts inside their alpha exteriors."

Noelle nodded. "He does have a soft heart. I see it when he interacts with his family. He's also very protective."

Brianne stood up. "Good. Now time to learn something. Stand up."

Noelle stood and waited for her next command.

"Okay, kneel on the floor, spread your knees, and put your hands behind your back. Stick out your breasts, Elle. You're offering your body to your Master. He owns it. Remember that. His will is supreme. Obedience brings him pleasure, and his pleasure is your only goal."

Noelle tried to relax into the pose. Brianne nodded.

"Look down at the floor. Some Masters like you to keep your eyes down. Very good. Okay, up on your feet. Next pose. Oh, this is fun. I've never trained a sub before."

Noelle rose to her feet. "Glad I could entertain you. Come on, be tough with me. I want to show him how serious I am."

Lisa stood up. "You'll need to curb your tongue, Elle. Masters like their subs quiet, in general. He may take away your permission to speak. Even if he doesn't, it's not a good idea to be chatty or sarcastic."

"If that's true, I'm in big trouble."

Brianne laughed. "Yep, you're going to get spanked on a regular basis. Welcome to the club, Elle!"

* * * *

Cam was nervous as hell, and he didn't like the feeling one little bit. He had spent the day distracted, wondering if Noelle would decide in his favor. By the end of the day, his nerves were stretched so taut he had been barking at everyone in sight. Even his usually happy-go-lucky brother had finally pulled him aside and told him to get his head out of his ass and lay off everyone.

"If you've got trouble with your woman, Cam, don't take it out on everyone around you. Go rub one out or whatever, but stop bein' an asshole."

Cam had snarked back that he wasn't the asshole, but decided in his mood he shouldn't be around anyone else. He had spent the rest of the day cleaning up the equipment barn, torturing himself with visions of Noelle sitting as far down the table as she could.

It was dinnertime now, and there was no more waiting. In a matter of moments, he would know what her decision was. If she didn't decide to give their relationship a chance, he wasn't sure what he would do. She was a woman he wanted in his life. He wanted to take their relationship to the next level. But she had to want it, too. He was asking a great deal of her. She was going to be way out of her comfort zone with him.

He sat down at the table as everyone gathered in the dining room. His favorite, pot roast, was being served, but he couldn't concentrate on anything but Noelle as she entered the room behind Abby. She looked beautiful in figure-hugging jeans that showed off her God-given curves and a white sweater that was the perfect backdrop for her glorious red hair. He would have thought she wasn't as nervous as he was except for the telltale chewing of her full bottom lip. She was gorgeous, and she had to be absolutely his. If she said no, he would just have to think of another plan.

She walked toward him and he held his breath. She dropped her eyes and his heart fell, then started beating a tattoo in his chest as she pulled out the chair to his right and sat down. He reached for her hand and gave it a squeeze. He could feel her trembling. She was as affected by the moment as he was. This amazing woman wanted to be his. To belong to him. A wave of possessiveness washed over him. He would make sure she never regretted her decision. He would be the Dom she needed. Cam hid his laughter.

The Dom she never even knew she wanted.

* * * *

She had made it through dinner. She just had to make it through the rest of the evening. Yes, there had been strange looks from the rest of the family when she had sat down at Cam's side and his hand had reached for hers. Abby had started to ask her a question only to be interrupted by Brody's commanding tone.

"No, Abby, not right now."

Noelle was now cowering in her bedroom after Abby and Julie had shooed her out of the kitchen when she tried to help with the dishes. She didn't regret saying yes to Cam, but she did wish she knew what was next. Lisa and Brianne had warned her about the loss of control going forward. She had to place her trust in Cam now. She was so lost in her thoughts she almost didn't hear the soft knock on the door.

"Noelle? It's Cam."

She scrambled off the bed and opened the door. Cam had a gentle smile on his face as if he understood the strain she was under with the others in the house.

"Let's go for a drive, sweetheart. I think we both need to get away from the loving arms and prying eyes of our family."

She couldn't agree more. She grabbed her purse and let him lead her down the stairs and into his SUV. She sat quietly in the passenger seat, biting her lip to keep from asking him where they were headed. She repeated to herself over and over, I have to trust him. Trust didn't come easily, but she would work on it. She smiled when they pulled up in front of the small log house where they had spent their first evening together. It was the perfect place to be alone.

Cam cupped her chin and turned her to face him. His large, callused hands were warm and gentle.

"Here's the key. Go on in and get comfortable. I just need to get a few things out of the back of the truck."

Noelle headed into the cozy cabin. This brought back the best of memories. Had it only been a few days ago she had met this man? Life could take a turn in a hurry.

She flipped on some lights and smiled. She had an idea, and she hoped he liked it. She knelt down on the soft rug near the fireplace and went into the pose Brianne had taught her. She wanted Cam to see she was really committed to doing this. She wanted him, just the way he was. She was determined she wouldn't try and change him. She understood this was a part of him. She heard the front door open and his steps halt in the doorway. She held her breath wondering if perhaps she shouldn't have done this, but then he entered the room the rest of the way. She heard him behind her, and then he was in front of her starting a fire in the fireplace. She was about to stand up when she felt his hand on her head, his fingers stroking her hair.

"This is a wonderful surprise, Noelle. Your submission is a treasure to me, something very precious. I will never take it for granted, and I will cherish it. Please know that I will always keep you safe and cared for."

He continued stroking her hair and then down her cheek, leaving a trail of heat where he touched.

"Where did you learn the slave pose, precious? Did Abby teach you?"

"No, Sir. Two of my friends in the book club are subs. They taught me today. You might say I had a crash course in submission from them. I wanted to please you, Sir."

He settled on the rug in front of her, raising her chin so she looked him in the eye.

"Well, you certainly pleased me. The only thing that would have pleased me more was if you were naked and in the slave pose." He lifted a long strand of hair and let it slip through his fingers. "God, your hair is amazing in this light. It's such a fiery combination of reds and golds. You're so beautiful. I'm very proud to call you my woman and submissive, Noelle. I'm humbled by your trust. Did you think I didn't notice that you didn't ask me where we were going?"

He had a lopsided grin, and she smiled back. He had noticed. "It wasn't easy, Sir, but I want to work on trusting you."

"We'll work on it together. From now on, you are never alone in this. You have me supporting you and helping you. Are comfortable calling me Sir? You may also call me Mr. Hunter when we are together like this."

Noelle nodded. "I think I will call you Sir. Mr. Hunter sounds like you're my high school gym teacher or something."

Cam laughed. "We definitely don't want that. Sir is fine and shows me respect. And yes, I expect you to slip up and call me by my name. Some Doms set standards so high their sub can never reach them. I believe in positive reinforcement. If you do things correctly, I reward you. It doesn't mean you will never be punished. It just means I'm not looking for opportunities to do so."

That's a relief.

"And so far, you've earned a big reward. Tonight I want to give you pleasure beyond anything you've ever experienced."

Noelle laughed. "Sounds like a plan, Sir. Oh shit, I'm supposed to stay quiet, aren't I? Hell, I'll never get this right."

Cam's deep laughter made her feel better. Perhaps she wasn't screwing this up as badly as she thought.

"I haven't told you any rules yet, pretty sub. So how do you know you're supposed to stay quiet? You can talk unless I take away your permission to speak, by the way. But I do have a rule about cursing. You'll need to clean up your language. Starting now."

"I'll try, Sir."

Cam shook his head. "No, pretty sub. You'll do more than try. You will clean up your language. It may take a few reminders in the form of a paddle on your perfectly shaped rear end, but you will succeed."

"So, that's one of your rules? Are there any others?"

Cam shrugged. "I don't have a bunch of rules you need to memorize. But I do have a few that I think are important. Ready to hear them?"

Noelle nodded vigorously. She needed to know what she was getting herself into.

Cam pulled her into his arms and lounged back against some cushions. He felt hard and hot, and she wanted to run her hands all over his yummy body. He didn't seem to be the strictest of Doms so far.

"I like the rules so far, Sir."

* * * *

Cam let his hands wander down his sub's body, slowly caressing her luscious curves. He wanted to savor this first time together. He wanted to make it memorable and special. This was the beginning of his campaign to show Noelle how wonderful it could be between them. She had already done her part in making it a night he wouldn't forget in a hurry. He had been shocked when he saw her on her knees waiting for him. His cock had instantly hardened and was now pressing insistently against his button fly, making rivet-sized dents in the flesh.

"We're going to start out easy tonight. Just a few rules to begin things. When we're together, just the two of us, I'm pretty easygoing. If we're at the club together, I'm much more formal about the rules."

Noelle lifted her head, her brow furrowed. He lifted a hand to smooth the lines from her forehead. He didn't want her worrying or thinking tonight. He wanted her relaxed and open.

"Are you worried about the club? There's a club in Bozeman I've frequented through the years. It caters to the lifestyle. I hope one day you might go with me. Don't worry, precious. We'll talk about everything. I can't take what you're not willing to give. That's the way this works."

To his relief, she smiled and laid her head back on his chest. He inhaled her soft fragrance that surrounded him. It was a combination of something floral and maybe a little baby powder. She smelled absolutely delicious. He couldn't wait to lick up her neck and nibble at her ear.

"Back to the rules. Generally, when we're in a scene, you need to be respectful and obey. Obedience is key. Call me Sir. Obey my commands. Don't use bad language. Don't touch me without permission. Don't come without permission. Don't worry if you don't know what to do. I'll direct you at all times. Just relax and go for the ride, so to speak. Other than that, I'll tell you if there's a specific rule I want you to follow."

Noelle's fingers were tracing circles on his chest sending sparks of heat straight to his aching cock. Perhaps he needed to command her to stop touching him now.

Fuck, no.

"That seems pretty straightforward. It's almost too easy."

Cam tangled his fingers in her silky hair and tugged her head back until her golden-brown eyes were gazing into his own.

"It won't be. You'll fight yourself to submit to me. Some of your instincts will be to rebel to see what I'll do about it. Your independence will rear its head and fight your desire to submit. It will be war. Don't doubt that, sweetheart. Time and trust will give you the confidence to allow yourself to submit to me and stop listening to all those voices in your head. Those voices are what we'll start working on tonight."

"Is that what they mean by subspace? When the voices shut up and leave you alone?"

Her eyes were wide but not with fear, with arousal. She was ready for their first time together.

"Yes, that's what they mean. We'll quiet those voices together. Starting now. Lie back on this rug with your hands over your head and your legs spread."

Noelle didn't move, as if she hadn't heard him. *Time to train her up.* He put just enough steel into his voice.

"Now."

This time Noelle scrambled into position, her breath coming in short pants. She was already climbing toward orgasm.

This is going to be fun.

* * * *

Noelle lay very still and tried to slow her breathing. She was painfully aroused, her pussy clenching, wanting to be filled, and her nipples beading, wanting to be licked and sucked. She tried to rein in her impatience. Cam had promised her pleasure like she had never known. He looked like a man who delivered on his promises. Just a glance at his hard cock outlined clearly through his jeans had her mouth watering. It would fill her pussy deliciously.

"I want you to stay very still. As still as you can, and stay as quiet as you can. Try not to make a sound. Concentrate on your breathing. It will help you stay focused."

Noelle relaxed her limbs and let her eyes flutter closed. He leaned over her and began running his hands down her body from her shoulders, over the aching tips of her breasts, down her belly, and toward her drenched cunt. She jerked up, his hands like iron brands through her clothes, sending fire licking along her veins and flowing straight to her clit. She moaned in arousal, the pleasure of finally feeling his hands on her body so intense.

"Easy, pretty sub. Lie still for me and stay very quiet. Focus, honey."

"Sorry, Sir. Sorry."

Her voice sounded hoarse and strained, and he had barely touched her. She was acutely aware she had already disobeyed him and they had just begun. It was embarrassing to be so weak-willed. Brianne and Lisa had warned her she would need to learn to be more disciplined.

He didn't reply, simply went back to caressing every part of her body but where she needed his hands the most. She squeezed her eyes shut, breathing in and out, trying to stay quiet and still.

"That's my girl. I'm proud of you. Are the voices quiet now?"

The voices were quiet. Somehow, while she was focusing on her breathing, staying quiet, and staying still, she had stopped listening to the voices in her head. For the first time in her adult life, she had allowed herself to just…be. She felt a little giddy in her triumph. Of course, the voices were coming back in full force, but she now knew she could turn them off if she really needed to.

"Yes, Sir. The voices stopped. They've started again, though."

He leaned close to her ear, his warm breath caressing her cheek.

"I know. I think your reward will quiet those voices. Now let's get these clothes off of you. You can't get your reward if you're not naked."

Yes, Sir.

Chapter Four

Cam pulled Noelle's sweater up and over her head and off, tossing it over his shoulder and onto an overstuffed chair. He caught his breath as her creamy skin was revealed inch by inch. Her generous breasts were covered by a flimsy lace bra, her rosy nipples clearly outlined. He ran the tip of his finger around the taut peaks, smiling as her back arched, and a moan slipped from between her lips. She was working hard to stay still and quiet. He really didn't care if she was successful. The exercise was only to quiet those loud, pesky voices in her head that kept her fighting her submissive urges.

He trailed his hands down her belly to the snap of her jeans, unfastening them, and pulled them down her legs. They joined her sweater on the chair. He held in his laughter, but couldn't stop his grin at her lacy lingerie paired with thick, woolen socks. Her feet must get cold easily.

"May I ask what's so amusing, Sir?"

Noelle looked down at herself with a frown. Cam pressed her back onto the rug with a chuckle.

"You are. Your submission is a treasure, your lingerie is sexy, and your socks make me smile."

Noelle giggled. "My feet get cold. I'm from Florida, you know."

"I know. From now on, it will be my duty, and my pleasure, to make sure these feet stay toasty warm. Let's get these thick socks off."

Cam quickly stripped off her socks and put one of her dainty feet on his thigh. He began to massage the soles and arches, drawing moans and groans as he found particularly sensitive spots. He cataloged each for future reference. He moved to her other foot and continued his tender, loving care. He wanted Noelle to see that a Dominant-submissive relationship was more than following orders, being spanked, and getting tied up. It was also about a Dominant cherishing and caring for their sub.

"Oh God, that feels so good."

Cam arched an eyebrow. "How does it feel, sub?"

"Sir. It feels so good, Sir."

Cam ran his fingers up her calf and was rewarded with goose bumps adorning her flesh.

"Good girl. It will come more easily as we progress. Now let's get you completely naked. I want to see my new sub without a stitch of clothing."

Noelle reached down to the butterfly fastening between her breasts, but he brushed her fingers away.

"My sub, my job. Aren't you supposed to be still and quiet?"

"Shit."

It was muttered under her breath, and she clearly didn't mean for him to hear it, but he did. He would have to do something about it. He couldn't lay down a rule and then do nothing when it was broken willfully.

"Noelle, what did you say?"

She bit her lip and looked guilty as all hell.

"Um, you mean just now?"

He leaned back on his heels, crossed his arms over his chest, and gave her a stern look.

"You're making this worse for yourself. What did you just say, sub?"

Her lip trembled.

"Shit. I said 'shit.' I'm very sorry, Sir."

"Thank you for apologizing. You know the rules, sweetheart, and you violated them. Your punishment will be a spanking."

Noelle's eyes went wide with shock, and she swallowed hard.

"A spanking? Just for cursing?"

He nodded. "I told you earlier what the penalty would be, if you remember. Since this is your first night, I won't use the paddle. But you will get a warmed bottom. It will help you remember to curb your language. Now, let's get your punishment over with so we can get back to the pleasure. Strip off the rest of your clothes and get on all fours on the rug."

Noelle started pulling her bra and panties off, revealing her beautiful breasts and the red triangle at the apex of her thighs. The reddish-gold curls were damp from her arousal, and Cam knew she was excited about her spanking, not fearful. He was going to love initiating his little sub with her first punishment. He rubbed his hands together in anticipation.

* * * *

Noelle braced herself on all fours on the rug. Despite being naked as the day she was born, she was plenty warm due to the fire in the fireplace and the fire in her pussy at the fantasy come to life of receiving a spanking from Cam's work-roughened hands.

In the position she was in, there was no way to be modest or try to cover any portion of her anatomy. It was all out there for his inspection. She knew her fair skin was flushed red with her embarrassment of being naked for the first time and being in this compromising position. She actually felt submissive to Cam as she knelt naked in front of the fireplace waiting for her punishment. He was standing now, walking around her, checking her out from every angle. He finally knelt next to her, reaching under her to play with her hard nipples, tweaking and rolling them. She gasped with the pleasure that shot straight to her already-hard and swollen clit.

"Your nipples are very sensitive, pretty sub. We'll have to try out some clamps on them."

The erotic thought sent cream pouring from her already-drenched pussy. She wiggled a little when his hand ran down her body and rubbed circles on her ass cheeks.

"Seems to me, you like the idea. Your thighs are shiny with your honey. Spread your knees a little, sweetheart. I want a taste of your sweet, little cunt."

Noelle muffled a moan as she slid her knees further apart. His callused fingers were right where she wanted them this time. He was running his fingers through her soaking pussy and playing with her clit. She whimpered when he removed his hand, but almost screamed his name when his tongue replaced it.

"Oh God, please, please."

The tongue pulled away, giving her clit the lightest of licks. The light touch was pure torture. She needed to come badly.

"How do you address your Dominant, sub?"

"Sir, oh, God, Sir, please, please lick me!"

She could feel his warm breath on her pussy and heard his chuckle.

"Sir will do, sub. Although calling me your God, and Lord and Master, might make me let you come sooner."

She scowled and was about to let him know what she thought of his statement when his tongue returned to her clit. She forgot everything she was going to say as he licked and nipped up and down her slit. She was floating in heaven when he pulled his mouth away. She protested, needing to come right now.

"No, sub. You will not come yet. Silence."

Steel laced his tone, and she bit her lip to stop the pleading words on the tip of her tongue. She was breathing heavy, and her arms already ached from holding herself in this position. His hands stroked down her spine and trailed down the crack of her ass to her back hole. She sucked in her breath as his fingers teased the opening.

"Have you ever been fucked here, Noelle? Have you had a man's cock here before?"

Noelle shook her head. She had been ordered to be silent.

"I'm going to fuck you here. I'll be the man who pops this cherry. Not tonight, but soon. You'll love my cock fucking you in the ass. You may end up loving it more than when I fuck your sweet pussy. It's the ultimate submission, having your ass breached, and you are going to give it to me, aren't you, my sub?"

Noelle nodded, feeling light-headed. She hadn't seen his cock yet, but the outline was large, and she wondered if her ass could actually take something so big. Yes, she was hungry for the experience. She wanted to give him everything, all of herself.

She didn't expect his hand to come down on her ass cheek hard and fast. She sucked in her breath as the heat from his hand spread through her abdomen and traveled to her pussy and clit. It came down a second time on the other cheek, the impact sending her rocking on her hands and knees. She steadied herself and waited. She didn't have to wait long. He gave her six more smacks, three on each ass cheek before pausing to rub her sore bottom. Honey was pouring from her cunt, and she had to steel herself not to beg for his cock. She was teetering on the edge of orgasm. If a breeze touched her clit, she knew she would fly apart.

"You do not have permission to come, sub. You need to control yourself. Focus, sweetheart. You can do it."

Noelle panted and shuddered. She tensed her muscles in an attempt to push back her arousal. He sat quietly next to her while she got control, rubbing her spanked ass and whispering encouraging words.

"Good girl, Noelle. I'm proud of you. Now tell me why you were punished."

"I used bad language."

She felt his warm lips kiss a wet trail down her spine.

"Very good. I don't think I can hold back much longer. Hold on, sweetheart. We're going for a ride."

She heard his zipper, the crinkle of a condom wrapper, then she felt the tip of his cock nudge at her pussy lips. The scent of his body and the heat of his skin overwhelmed her senses. He pressed forward, his cock stretching her pussy wide and rubbing against sensitive spots in her cunt she never knew she had. His cock was so large it seemed to take forever, but he was finally in to the hilt. She felt the rough hair on his thighs brush hers and the warmth of his body pressing against her sore ass cheeks. She bent forward and pressed herself back on his dick, loving how he filled every part of her. He ran his hand up her back and tangled it in her hair, tugging her head back as his other hand anchored her hip.

"Let's go, baby."

* * * *

Cam was balls deep in his sexy sub, her pussy enfolding him in its wet heat. He had never felt anything so sublime, and it was playing hell with his so-called iron control. He pulled out slowly, leaving just the head in her cunt, before pressing slowly back in.

Noelle wiggled her ass and moaned. She wanted him to speed up and fuck her fast and hard. He planned to, but not quite yet.

"Easy, pretty sub. You'll get what you need, but you have to be patient."

He needed to be patient, too. He wanted to pound her hard, but she was extremely tight and he didn't want to hurt her or make her sore tomorrow. He had a high sex drive, and he wanted to be able to make love to her over and over without guilt. It was his duty and pleasure to care for her and keep her safe.

He began thrusting in and out, slowly, carefully, his hand holding her hair to keep her still. She was panting. Her skin turned a rosy hue, highlighted by the firelight. She pushed her ass up in the air and leaned down on her elbows, her cheek against the rug. Her eyes were half-closed in ecstasy, and he felt a surge of emotion that he was the one bringing her such intense pleasure. A moan escaped from between her pouty lips.

"Please, Sir! Please let me come!"

He began to speed up his thrusts, her cunt so wet, he slid in and out easily. He was pounding her pussy hard and fast now, and he smacked her ass, tugging on her hair as she met each thrust with abandon. He looked down at the pale skin of her bottom, his handprint a red splotch on her already-pinkened skin. He smacked her again, and her breathing sped up, the sounds she made becoming more urgent. He felt the pressure build in his lower back and knew he couldn't hold back much longer. He reached under her and ran circles around her swollen clit.

"Come, sub."

He used his best Dom voice, and she immediately responded. Her pussy clamped down on his cock and for a moment she froze before her body started to shudder and tremble. He could feel the ripples on his cock, and it was all he needed to send himself over. His orgasm seemed to explode from his balls and out his cock. He came hard, his body rocked with the power of his climax. He slumped over her back as the tension drained from his body, leaving him grinning and satisfied. His woman was amazing, and she was all his.

He pulled gently from her body and quickly took care of the condom, returning with a warm cloth to clean her sticky thighs. He tossed it away and pulled her close, tugging a quilt draped on a chair over them. He held her as their breathing slowed and their heartbeats returned to normal. Her cheek was pressed against his chest, and he stroked her hair, letting the silky strands run through his fingers. She seemed content to cuddle and let the silence surround them for a long time.

Eventually, Noelle started to fidget, and he let her pull away to gaze into her soft amber eyes. She swallowed hard. It looked like she wanted to say something. He stayed quiet and let her find the words.

"I'm...I'm submissive. I really, honest to God, wasn't sure until a few minutes ago. But, I'm submissive. I have to say it because it's true."

He ran his finger down her smooth cheek, loving how soft her skin was to his touch. *What a brave little sub.* He loved how she faced this head-on, not pretending, although he knew she would grapple more with her submissive nature. She was a strong woman, and giving up control wasn't going to come easy for her.

"I'm so proud of you, Noelle. I know this can't be easy for you. You're a strong, independent woman. I don't want to change that about you. I want you to still feel in control of your life, but offer you the opportunity to let go and trust someone else to care for you. I want our relationship to add to your life, not subtract from it."

This wasn't something to bully her into. This was something she had to want.

Noelle nodded, her expression calm and resolute. "I don't feel too brave right about now, but I'm glad you think so. I'm not calling a halt to this. I want to try. Specifically, I want to try with you."

Cam pulled her close and cuddled his woman to his heart. He was in dangerous territory with this courageous, wonderful woman. She had only promised him a few weeks, not a lifetime. Already she was so much more than a submissive. She was becoming his heart.

Chapter Five

Noelle's eyes fluttered open, and she stifled a yawn. She and Cam had fallen asleep in front of the fireplace after their earth-shattering sex. She smiled as she remembered their passion and how hard she had come. She'd never had her world rocked anywhere near that intense before. Cam was amazing in and out of bed.

"You're wearing a very witchy smile on your face, Noelle. Care to share your thoughts?"

Cam's deep voice rumbled in his chest, and his warm breath tickled her brow. She pushed herself up and looked into his sky-blue eyes. They were soft and warm tonight, and she could easily lose herself in their depths. This man was more than any she had ever met.

She ran her hand up his bare chest. "Just remembering the naughty things we did a few hours ago. It was pretty awesome, if you want to know the truth. Can we do it again, Sir?"

Cam chuckled and sat up to tend the fire which had burned low while they slept.

"Go easy on me, little sub. I'm older than you, you know."

Noelle eyed his already-hard and straining cock. He had more control and stamina than most men she knew or heard about. By rights he should be sprawled out on the floor, snoring until morning.

"You don't act older than me. In fact, I'm not sure I believe you about being forty-nine. Are you sure?"

"Positive. Aren't you turning thirty in a few weeks? We'll have to have a birthday party."

Noelle pushed at his shoulder playfully. "Doesn't the big, bad Dom know not to remind a lady of her age? I could be frightfully sensitive about it."

She laughed out loud as his expression turned to dismay.

"Hey, it's okay. I was just teasing you. I'm not sensitive about it at all. Age is just a number."

Cam shook his head, but still didn't look relieved. "Are you sure? Shit, I didn't even think. Thirty seems pretty young to me, that's all. I'm going to be fifty in six months if you want to tease me about it."

Noelle snuggled into the cushions and blankets. "You don't seem too concerned about it. It doesn't bother you, does it?"

"It didn't until I met an amber-eyed, red-haired sub who drives me crazy and is twenty years younger than me. You looked at me like I was a senior citizen when you found out I was Brody's dad."

Noelle felt a warmth build somewhere in the vicinity of her heart. He was actually concerned about whether she thought he was old.

"I don't care about your age. I was just surprised. That's all. Besides, my friends say I'm an old fart sometimes. I don't like to go to clubs and bars. I work most of the time, since I run my own business. My idea of a wild night is dinner and a movie with my friends. I've been on my own since I was eighteen. I think I'm pretty mature for my age."

Cam gave her a long look. "Eighteen is pretty young. Didn't you go to college?"

Noelle's lips twisted in a grimace. This was a tough subject. It wasn't that she didn't want to tell him. It was just that no one came out of this story looking too good.

"I did. Art school. My parents were not happy about it. In fact, they were furious. I had done well in high school and won a scholarship to a small, private college in southern Florida that they approved of and wanted me to attend. They hoped I would become a lawyer. I'm not sure why as both my parents are teachers. They just have this thing about me being an attorney. But, I had entered an art contest. They didn't know about it. I won and also received a scholarship to an art school in New York. They were furious."

Noelle paused. It was still a painful story to tell.

"Listen, I wasn't the easiest child to raise. As you may have noticed, I'm a little impetuous and stubborn. My grandmother said I had a zest for life. My parents called me a hellion. There wasn't anything I didn't think I could do, and I drove my poor parents crazy proving them wrong on practically a daily basis."

Cam gave her a shrewd look. "Were they wrong?"

Noelle stared up at the ceiling. "Yes, a lot of the time. They wanted a quiet, well-behaved daughter like Abby. She always did what she was told. She didn't sneak out of the house in the middle of the night to go cave exploring in the middle of Florida. She didn't sign up for a chance to win a race car lesson. She didn't go bungee jumping off a bridge. Boy, were they pissed about that. My parents say I made them old before their time."

"It sounds like you do have a zest for life. You also sound like Caden. He wants to experience everything life has to offer. And yes, sometimes it's tough to be his parent."

"I know. I was a rotten kid, I guess. So when I told my parents I wasn't going to be a lawyer, I was going to be an artist, well, they felt betrayed. I might as well have said I was running away to work in a carnival. It was the last straw for them."

Cam held up his hand. "Now, wait a minute. I never said Caden was a rotten kid. He was just a challenging kid. You weren't rotten, either, Noelle. You just had parents that didn't know how to handle you, that's all. I'm sure they're proud of you now."

Noelle shook her head. "You don't understand. I had to sneak away to go to school in New York. I left in the middle of the night, leaving a note behind. My parents forbade me to go. They said they would only pay for college if I became a lawyer. So, I packed my bags, my life savings, and my old car and headed for New York after they fell asleep one night. They were livid then, and they've never really put it behind them. Every holiday I hear about how my life could have been so much better, if only I had listened to them."

Cam blinked in confusion. "Wait a minute. You left for New York on your own? How in the hell did you live then? Did the scholarship pay living expenses?"

"No, just tuition and books. I got a job as a waitress. I waited tables through school and had five roommates. New York was amazing, and I don't regret a moment of it. I entered a lot of art contests, and that money helped, too. By the time I came home to live and start my business, they'd cooled down some. But they've never really forgiven me."

Cam scraped a hand down his face. "They left you to fend for yourself? Fuck, Noelle, I'm proud as hell of you for taking care of yourself. Working hard and going to school isn't easy. It just underlines for me just how stubborn and independent you are. I admire what you've done. Abby tells us that you're very successful and sought after for your designs. Your parents will come around, I'm sure."

Noelle felt the heat in her cheeks. Her friends had told her they were proud of her, but coming from this man, it meant so much more. His opinion shouldn't mean this much, so soon. But it did. She was glad he admired what she did. She was proud of herself, too.

"Maybe they will. I've learned to live without their approval. My own approval is the most important thing. I'm proud of what I've accomplished. I'm proud of what I've done here tonight with you. I was able to put my trust in you and submit. I know you probably don't think it's a big deal, but for me it's huge."

Cam shook his head firmly. "You're wrong. I know what a big deal it is for you. I'm humbled by the trust you've placed in me."

"A Dom humble? Isn't that a contradiction?"

"If a Dom isn't humbled by the gift of submission, he doesn't have any business being a Dom. You don't owe me anything, Noelle. I can't take anything you aren't willing to give me. That's how this works."

Noelle felt a lump in her throat forming. It only made her trust him more with this delicious combination of gratitude and domination. She felt the urge to make a statement to him about how she was feeling. She may have only promised him a short time, but she wanted it to be filled with how she felt tonight, at this moment.

Noelle dropped the blanket and pressed her body against his hot, hard chest.

"I want to try everything with you. Push my boundaries, tie me up, gag me, spank me. Do whatever you want to me. I want to experience everything with you."

* * * *

This woman was a revelation. So spirited, so independent, yet soft as butter inside. She needed a strong man to protect her tender heart. It was clear her parents had wounded her with their callous attitude. He wouldn't mind a few minutes with her parents. They needed their eyes opened to what a treasure they had in Noelle.

Cam's fingers trailed up her delicate spine and threaded through her long hair. "Your impetuous nature is showing, pretty sub. It takes years of trust and working together to experience everything. But I can give you a taste of the life while you're here. Nothing too extreme, but some variety."

Noelle sighed. "I love it when the voices are quiet."

Cam stroked her hair. "What do the voices say, sweetheart?"

She snuggled closer. "A lot of 'shoulds.' I should work harder. I should visit my parents more. I should have been an attorney. I should go to church every Sunday. I should have been married and had kids by now. Stuff like that. So annoying."

"That's a lot of 'shoulds.' Do you know what your Dom says you should do?"

He heard her giggle, and his heart did a flip in his chest.

"No, what does he say?"

"He says you should kiss your way down to my cock and give it some oral love."

She gave him a mischievous grin. "Yes, my Lord and Master."

Cam cracked up. She had remembered what he said earlier. She wanted to come sooner, rather than later. Well, he liked to reward good behavior.

Her warm lips kissed a damp trail down his belly and straight to his cock, leaving the skin tingling wherever she touched. Her tongue flicked out to lick the drop of pre-cum on the crown of his dick, and he groaned at the erotic sight.

"How do I taste, little sub?"

She licked her lips, and her eyes glowed with passion.

"Yummy, salty. I want more, please, Sir."

"You can play for a while, but I have other ideas of where I'm going to come, sweetheart."

She bent her head and engulfed the head of his cock in her mouth. It felt like wet velvet surrounding him, and his hand reflexively grabbed her hair and tangled in it, tugging her closer so his cock slid farther into her wet warmth.

"Fuck, baby, that feels like heaven."

He threw his head back and closed his eyes, enjoying the sensation of her mouth and tongue servicing him. He reached down and pinched her nipples, making her moan despite the man meat stuffed in her mouth. The vibrations went straight down his dick and pulled his balls tighter. He was going to shoot his load if she kept this up. He pulled his cock from her mouth, despite her protests.

"No, baby. I have something else in mind."

It had been his fantasy since he'd laid eyes on her in his T-shirt in this very cabin. He was going to live out the fantasy now.

"Lie down on your back, hands over your head, holding on to the chair legs. I'm going to rub some lotion between your bountiful breasts and fuck you there."

He grinned at her shocked expression. He was looking forward to shocking her some more while she was here in Montana.

* * * *

He wanted to do what? She was pretty sure what he was talking about wasn't possible. He must be suffering from lack of sleep. She opened her mouth to object, when his hand came down on her thigh with a smack.

"Now, sub. I don't like having to repeat my commands. Lie down."

He practically growled the words, and she scrambled into position, her thigh hot where he had punished her for ignoring him. She needed to learn to listen better or she was going to be sporting a sore ass 24-7. She reached up and held a chair leg in each hand, settling herself on the rug in front of the fire. He had a bottle of lotion he had pulled from the bag, and he was watching her with a remote expression.

"Stay still. I want you to try to not move. Just because I asked you to."

Noelle swallowed the lump in her throat and nodded. She desperately wanted to please him. She wasn't sure where this emotion came from, but it was real. She may not want her parents' approval, but she damn sure wanted his. She wanted to be the best sub he'd ever had.

"Yes, Sir."

"Good girl. Silence now, Noelle."

She took some deep breaths to slow her pounding heart. His hands were sliding all over her body, igniting a fire inside her. Flames licked along her sensitized skin and she wanted to throw herself at him and beg him to fuck her hard. Her pussy was dripping honey and her nipples were painfully tight. She needed his cock inside her, riding her, rubbing her clit and sending her to paradise. She bit her lip to stem the begging that was certain to come out if he continued much longer.

Relief relaxed her muscles as his caresses stopped. Instead, he squeezed the lotion bottle and two large dollops landed in the valley between her breasts. The lotion was cold, and she jumped at the sensation.

Cam scowled. "Stay still, Noelle. Every time you disobey me, you delay your own release. This is your Dominant's fantasy. I've been fantasizing about doing this to you since our first night here in the cabin."

He reached down and smeared the lotion, then straddled her body, his cock nestled between her breasts. It was starting to dawn on her how this was going to work. Her pussy clenched as she realized she wouldn't be getting fucked there. Her ample chest was going to provide the pussy.

His hands caressed her breasts and tweaked the nipples.

"I love these tits. So round and full. They overflow my hands, and the skin is so soft and smooth. When I push them together, it's going to make a warm, snug cunt for me to fuck."

True to his word, he pushed them together, and his cock slid right in. His fingers plucked at her nipples, while he slid his cock in and out of the tight channel. The lotion made his thrusts painless, but the twin sensations of pinched nipples and his cock stroking her skin was making her pant and moan. One look at his face showed how much he was enjoying her body. His teeth were clenched, and the cords of his neck stood out as he held himself back, drawing out the pleasure.

His thrusts sped up, and she knew he was close. She gripped the chair to stop herself from grabbing his tight, muscled ass as he powered into her.

"Fuck, fuck, fuck, fuck. Touch me, baby."

His muttered words came right before he froze, letting her breasts go. She reached down and grabbed his hard cock, her hands moving up and down the velvety skin.

His cum spurted from the tip, and she lifted her head to close her mouth over the head of his cock. She swallowed every drop of his hot load before sinking back onto the carpet with a grin on her face. Her badass Dom looked shattered, his eyes glazed over with passion.

She was shocked at how quickly he shook it off, giving her an evil smile. "Dammit, sub. I was going to come on your breasts, not in your mouth. Did I tell you to put my cock in your mouth, Noelle?"

She shook her head, still grinning. He wasn't really mad. "No, Sir. You did not. It was my idea, Sir."

He quirked an eyebrow at her. "Still fighting submission, are you? Well, I certainly can't spank you again tonight or you won't be able to sit down for a week. But I think I can come up with something else to remind you who calls the shots around here. Roll over and put your ass in the air, sub."

She knew to be obedient this time, rolling over and presenting her bottom. She heard him rummage in his bag.

"You'll wear this butt plug until morning as a reminder of who makes the rules."

She peeked at the clock on the wall. One in the morning. She felt drops of wetness on her backside. Lube.

Fuck.

He let the lube trickle down her crack, and she heard his chuckle as she jumped. The lube was cold. If it hadn't been a punishment, maybe he would have warmed it first.

He ran his finger over the tight, puckered rosette, and she was already thinking about the day his cock would breach it. This plug would be the first step in stretching her so she could take him more comfortably. He pressed it to her back hole.

"Relax and breathe, Noelle. Push out with your muscles."

He worked the tip into the small orifice, pushing gently but insistently. She was wiggling her ass, her bottom tingling. She'd never had any attention centered here. He swatted her bottom to get her attention.

"Stop moving around so much, Noelle. Now push out. It will make this easier."

She pushed out and was surprised when the plug slid right in. He hadn't been kidding. She'd felt a stretch, but no burn. Her ass simply felt full. She couldn't imagine how it would feel to have his big cock up there. He'd split her in two, for heaven's sake. She shook her ass but couldn't dislodge it. It was in there until he took it out.

His fingers traced patterns on her ass cheeks. "I wish you could see what I see, Noelle. It's an erotic sight to see the plug peeking out of your ass cheeks, knowing I'll be there soon. Not tonight, but soon enough."

He pressed a finger in her wet, waiting pussy, and she cried out at the sensation. She felt needy, almost desperate.

"Someone needs to come. Lie back down and hold your legs open. I'm going to eat your pussy until you scream."

Yes, Sir!

* * * *

He ran his fingers through her drenched cunt and then pressed two fingers into her tight pussy. Being inside her was heaven, but he had rode her hard earlier. He didn't want to make her sore. He would save that pleasure for another time.

He added a third finger, her cunt so wet they slid in easily. He found her G-spot and hooked his fingers so they rubbed it with each stroke. Noelle responded immediately, her face and chest flushed with arousal, her head thrashing back and forth as she moaned and whimpered. She'd been through so much tonight, and she'd submitted more than he expected. He decided to put her out of her misery.

He trailed his fingers down her slit to the end of the plug, giving it a twirl and pulling it out about halfway, before thrusting it back in. Her body reacted like it had been hit by electricity. Her muscles went taut, her toes curled, and she screamed his name.

"Sir! Please, Sir!"

He lowered his head and licked her cunt from opening to clit, continuing to play with the plug. She was aroused by the ass play. She was going to love having a cock there, rubbing all those dark nerves.

He kept up his tongue play until she was moaning and panting, her pleading like music to his Dom ears.

"Come, Noelle."

He closed his mouth over her hard, swollen clit, scraping his teeth slightly on the sides. She screamed one last time before gushing cream all over his hand, her pussy milking his fingers. He let her come down gently, until she was a mass of Jell-O in his arms. He pulled her close and kissed her forehead.

"Like that, sweetheart? You seem to like having me eat your pussy."

She looked up at him through her thick, dark lashes. "I love it, Sir. Your mouth is dangerous. Very dangerous."

He chuckled. "The only dangerous thing that might happen is for you to come without permission. That would get you a punishment. One you probably won't like."

She wriggled against him. "I'm still in the middle of my last punishment. I don't suppose—"

He shook his head. The beginning with a new sub was an important time. He needed to show her he wasn't a pushover. He didn't tolerate topping from the bottom. He'd heard, from his brother and sons no less, he was too strict. She'd just have to get used to him.

"Uh-uh. You take your punishment like a big girl. It stays until morning. I need to start stretching you anyway. Perhaps, I'll have you wear a plug all the time."

She started to protest, then shut her mouth, thinking better of it.

"Good girl. You're learning. I'm in charge. I make the rules. Now let's get some sleep. I'll carry you into the bedroom."

She grabbed his arm. "You'll throw your back out."

He gave her a look that told her what he thought of that remark.

"I am not that damn old, sub. This might be a good time to be silent like your friends told you."

He laughed as Noelle pressed her lips together, pretended to lock her mouth closed, and throw away the invisible key.

"We'll see how long that lasts."

He lifted her, cuddling her close to his heart. His cock was already reinflating. He decided sleep was still a long way away. He'd have her again in the bedroom. He couldn't get enough of her.

Chapter Six

"These invitations are so pretty. They have so much more to choose from than when I got married."

Julie sipped her coffee while helping fold, stuff, and address wedding invitations. Abby smiled as she carefully placed tissue paper between the pages. "Aren't they gorgeous with the gold lettering? I was glad to have your and Noelle's help picking them out. Brody's wonderful, but hasn't been much help with the wedding preparations."

Noelle licked an envelope, making a face. "That's why I'm here, isn't it? To help with all the things that your macho fiancé isn't interested in?"

Julie sighed. "Colt was useless when I was planning our wedding. He would have been happy if we had a cookout and served hot dogs and beer at the reception. Luckily, my mother helped. In fact, if I remember correctly, she bullied me into a few decisions I don't think I would have made on my own. Pink bridesmaid dresses were one of them."

Abby gave Noelle a sly smile. "Maybe we'll have another wedding sometime soon. You never know."

Noelle didn't pretend to not know what Abby was talking about. She and Cam had been spending a great deal of time together the last week. That next night, after their time at the cabin, Cam had pulled her into his bedroom to spend the night. She was still there. She had moved her things into his room the next day. He was determined they wouldn't hide from the family. Their relationship was out in the open and apparently celebrated. Everyone had been giving them smiles when they would see her and Cam holding hands. Well, everyone but Julie and Colt's eighteen-year-old son, John. He had a perpetual sullen look on his face. For a young man a few months from graduating from high school, he didn't seem all that happy. About anything.

Noelle, however, was ecstatic. The last week with Cam had been amazing. She would find herself smiling and humming for no particular reason. She wanted to bake cookies because she found out he liked chocolate chip cookies. She wanted to rub his shoulders after his long day working on the ranch. She wanted to rip his clothes off of him and have her wicked way with his gorgeous body with its tan skin, and rippling muscles.

He was a strict, but fair Dom. Showing her how to turn off the voices in her head, and find deep pleasure in her submission. She loved getting spanked, and she couldn't wait to be restrained. He was the most amazing lover, his imagination and technique never failing to bring her to the heights of passion.

Noelle tossed another envelope on to the pile. "Subtle, Ab. Very subtle. Cam and I have only known each other a week. It's a tad early to shop for a dress and name our children."

Abby waved her hand. "I knew Brody was the one the minute I met him. You don't need to know someone for years to know if you want to spend your life with them. We're not in high school, after all."

"That's what my friend, Lisa, said. You knew right away? And I have a reputation for being impetuous. What about you, Julie? Did you know right away?"

Julie smiled at the memory. "We were in high school, actually. Colt and Cam were stars on the football team. All the girls wanted to date them. They were too popular and way too handsome for their own good. So of course I had a crush, too. Colt's locker was just a few down from mine, and I was flirting with him all the time, but he never asked me out. Finally, I accepted a date with Steve Storm, a friend of Colt's. He was jealous and ended up punching Steve out at a party. Colt and I have been together since."

Abby laughed. "Steve Storm? What a great name!"

Noelle joined in. "Sounds like a porno name. Whatever happened to him anyway?"

Julie gave them a smug look. "He's the principal at the high school. But he still looks great. He could do porn if he wanted to."

They were all laughing when the front door opened and they heard the click of high heels on the maple wood floors. Noelle was surprised to see the normally smiling and easygoing Julie frown at their female visitor. She was tall and slender, with pale blonde hair and golden tan skin. Noelle inwardly grimaced, knowing her own skin would never turn that lovely shade in the sun. Redheads weren't meant to sunbathe.

Julie stood up, her lips tight.

"Gwen, we weren't expecting you. What can I do for you?"

The beautiful blonde had a smile that was less than genuine.

"I came to talk to my sons. I need one of them to come over and hang my new drapes. Where are they?"

"Out on the ranch, of course. You remember Abby, don't you? And this is her sister, Noelle. She's come to help with the wedding."

Gwen ignored Abby and Noelle, frowning at Julie. "Lucas said they would be working near the house this afternoon."

Noelle was busy taking in this surprise visit and didn't hear John coming in the front door, home from school. He burst into the kitchen, dropping his backpack, grabbing a soda from the refrigerator, and coming to an abrupt halt when he saw Gwen. His face turned very red and he gazed at his shoes intently.

Gwen studied him for a moment, giving him a nod, before turning back to the women. She set her purse down on the counter, and it seemed like she might be settling in to wait. Julie looked as if she was going to have none of it.

"Gwen, does Cam know you're here?"

For someone so beautiful, Gwen could get an ugly look on her face.

"I don't tell my ex-husband my comings and goings, Julie. I was done doing that fifteen years ago." Her fingers traced a line around her neck. "I don't wear his collar anymore. He can't tell me what to do."

"I never could. You were defiant then, as now."

Cam's deep tones had Noelle turning in surprise to the back door. Cam and Colt were stomping into the kitchen, their expressions grim. Cam was not happy about seeing his ex-wife. She was surprised when he came up behind her and placed his hands on her shoulders, the warm weight reassuring.

Gwen pursed her lips and looked bored.

"I need one of the boys to come to my house and help me hang some curtains. Send Brody."

Cam shook his head. "No. Brody is at the outskirts of the ranch right now. When he gets back, he'll be spending time with his fiancée, Abby. Did you greet Abby, Gwen? She's going to be your daughter-in-law."

"I'm sure I must have." Gwen's eyes narrowed on Cam's hands. "And who might this be? Your new sub? She's...delightful, darling. But a trifle young for you, don't you think? Are you going through a midlife crisis, Cam? So sad, you feel you need to prove your manhood in such a manner."

Noelle started to rise and tell this bitch on wheels off. She had the temper to match her hair color. Cam's fingers tightened just slightly, pressing her into her chair.

"I don't need to prove anything, Gwen. I'm pretty secure these days. This is Noelle, Abby's sister and yes, my girlfriend and sub. I'll send Lucas to your house in the morning around nine."

Gwen picked up her purse. "Make it ten, darling. I like to sleep in."

John finally stopped staring at the floor. He lifted his head, and pushed his cowboy hat back on his head.

"I can go now, Cam."

Cam started to object, but then turned to Colt, who just shrugged.

"If you want to go, son, I guess that would be okay. Gwen, are you okay with John helping?"

Gwen smiled at John and linked her arm with his. "Of course. Any big, strong man will do."

Cam pulled a set of keys off the pegboard near the door and tossed them at John.

"Take the truck, John, and whatever tools you need from the garage. And thanks."

Miraculously, John almost smiled. "Thanks, Uncle Cam. I'll be careful."

Everyone in the kitchen was silent as John and Gwen headed toward the front door. Finally, Cam spoke.

"Gwen, next time? Call first."

* * * *

Cam placed his toothbrush back in the holder on the bathroom counter and padded back into the bedroom. Noelle was leaning back on a pile of pillows, glasses perched on her cute nose, completely engrossed in her e-reader. Her hair was in disarray, curling around her shoulders and face from her shower just minutes ago. She was wearing his favorite University of Montana T-shirt and had to admit it looked way better on her. The shirt stopped just midthigh on her shapely legs. Her toes were painted a bright red and made him want to take each one in his mouth, sucking and driving her wild while she was restrained and unable to stop him.

He loved having her in his bed. Fuck, who was he kidding? He loved having her in his life. Period. The last week had been the best he could remember. She liked to tell dirty jokes and make him laugh. They didn't agree on politics, and she loved to debate him. She liked to cook, and dinner each night had been a festival for his taste buds. She made melt-in-the-mouth pancakes for breakfast using bacon for the smiley face. She drove her sensible sedan too fast down his dirt road, which he hated, and encouraged his sons to think about taking chances to have the future they wanted, which he liked.

Of course, the nights were their time together. Her submission was sweeter than any he had known. Just knowing how difficult it was for her made it so much more special. She had taken to a D/s relationship like a duck to water. If anything, she thought he was moving too slow. She was already trying to top from the bottom by suggesting things he might want to do to her. She was reading way too many of those erotic books with her friends.

He hadn't used restraints on Noelle. Yet. He wanted her to be able to feel comfortable with him and be able to trust him absolutely. Submission had to be slowly earned. It couldn't be demanded or taken by force. He hoped tonight would be the turning point for them. He was going to give his pretty little sub a safe word tonight when he tied her to the bed. He couldn't wait to see her naked and spread eagle for his pleasure. And hers, too, of course.

He fell back on the bed with a sigh. He worked hard during the day, and slept like a rock at night. He loved working his ranch, and having the feeling of satisfaction knowing he was building a legacy for his children.

Noelle studiously avoided his eyes, keeping them trained on her reader.

"Ignoring me, Noelle, isn't going to stop us from having the discussion we need to have. We need to talk about Gwen."

She looked up and pulled the glasses from her nose. "We don't have to do this. I don't need you to explain something that happened years ago. Frankly, after meeting her today, I can't imagine you married to her, let alone her submitting to you."

Cam chuckled. His honest little sub never varnished the truth. "First, of all, I know I don't have to talk to you about it. But if we're going to be Dominant and submissive and also man and woman, we need to be honest about the things that made us who we are. My marriage to Gwen changed me. Fuck, I hope for the better. But I definitely grew up."

Noelle smiled. "You said 'fuck.' Do I get to give you a spanking?"

"No, but now I get to give you one since you said 'fuck.' I'm proud of you, by the way. Your language has improved in the last week."

Noelle pouted. "The Dom-sub stuff isn't fair. You get to use bad language and I don't."

Cam lay back with his hands behind his head. "That's why I like being the Dom. I like to make the rules."

He gave her a mock frown. "As I was saying, I don't have to tell you, but I want to. If we're going to be in a relationship together, no matter how temporary, you're going to need to understand my marriage, and divorce, to Gwen. Also, Gwen is a sub. Of sorts. She likes to top from the bottom. She's also into pain. More pain than I like to dish out. It was a source of contention between us. One of many."

Noelle frowned. "She *likes* pain? She wanted you to hurt her? Like bleeding or something?"

"No, not bleeding. But Gwen likes a good, hard whipping with a single tail. I don't mind using a single tail on occasion, but it's never been my favorite thing. I don't like anything more than a light to medium flogging."

Noelle rolled her eyes. "Just a flogging, huh? I'm so fu—uh, freakin' relieved."

"You should be, and good catch, sweetheart. But, back to the subject at hand. Me and Gwen. She and I met in college. She wanted to date a football star. She was pretty and seductive, and I was just some dumb country boy who liked girls who chased him. I thought I was a real hotshot, getting a sports scholarship and having girls hanging around me all the time. But Gwen was smarter than most of those girls. She was playing for keeps."

Noelle sat up, the frown back on her pretty face. "You were a fucking football star in college? Julie said you were a star in high school, but college is a whole different thing."

"That's one, little sub. You didn't know because I don't talk about it and also because I'm guessing you weren't even born at the time. I was a football star at college. I never made it to the pros. Something Gwen never let me forget. I blew my knee out my senior year. I can tell when it's going to rain now. It'll start aching and acting up."

"So you played football, dated Gwen, and then blew out your knee. How did you end up marrying her?"

"She was the first girl I dated that really embraced the whole Dominant-submissive thing. I had dated other girls who just played at it. They didn't mind a little spanking or maybe tying their hands now and then, but they weren't truly submissive. I realized they weren't enjoying it like I did. Gwen was different. But in my inexperience, I mistook her masochism for submission. She's slightly submissive. She wants someone to take control of sex as long as they don't push her limits. She does want someone to hurt her. Something she pushed me to do more and more as the years passed. But in the beginning, it wasn't too bad."

"You're saying it took more and more pain to make her happy?"

Cam's jaw tightened. "More pain and less submission with each passing year. It got to the point that when we went to the club, I had another Dom use the whip on her. I couldn't stand to hurt her that much. Later, she would taunt me for not being man enough to give her what she wanted. She needed pain to feel submissive. When I couldn't give her the kind of pain she needed, she stopped being submissive to me."

"So that's why you divorced? She wouldn't be submissive?"

Cam shook his head. "No. We divorced because I found out she was having an affair with a Dom from the club. A Dom who could give her what she needed."

Cam watched Noelle's face closely. Hopefully, she valued fidelity the way he did. Her eyes went wide with surprise and her mouth hung open.

"She was unfaithful? To you?"

Cam pulled her close and dropped a kiss on the top of her head. "Yes, pretty girl, she was unfaithful. To me. I'm glad to see you don't approve of that kind of behavior."

Noelle shook her head in disbelief. "I can't imagine anyone being unfaithful to you. You're the best lover I've ever—"

Cam put his hand over her mouth. "Stop. As much as I love hearing how hot in the sack I am, I do not want to hear about any men before me. I know there were men, but I sure as fuck don't need to be reminded. I'm a possessive, mean Dom."

Noelle laughed and pulled a face. "Possessive? Yes. Mean? No. Strict? Awfully. I really miss cursing."

Noelle sighed dramatically, and Cam felt a tug in his heart. This tiny little redhead was trouble with a capital *T*. And damn, if he didn't enjoy every minute of it.

"I'm not backing down on the cursing. Think of it as character building."

Noelle rolled her eyes. "More like submission building. I may be submissive, oh Lord and Master, but I'm not dumb. I'm onto you, just so you know."

Cam felt his cock harden. He dreamed of the day she might call him Master, but not in jest. He was already thinking about a collar around her neck. He just had to convince her he was worth it.

"I never thought any different."

Noelle plucked at the comforter. "So, you divorced her because of the other Dom?"

"We didn't just divorce over the infidelity, although that was a major issue. We disagreed about everything. Gwen wanted me to sell the ranch. She wanted to live in leisure, and she hated being so isolated out here. She wasn't very maternal, either. I would have happily had more children, but she was done after the boys. I liked to curl up after a long day, and she wanted to go into town and go to the club. We just never meshed honestly. We struggled from the beginning. Frankly, the affair was just the excuse we both needed to call it quits. She may not have been Mother of the Year, but she loved the boys and wanted the best for them."

"The boys live with you."

Cam nodded, remembering those first years after the divorce. "Yes. As I said, Gwen wanted the best for the boys, so she agreed they should live here on the ranch with me. They visited her in town on the weekends, and we shared holidays. It was tough on the boys in the beginning. I think they thought we might get back together. Brody was ten, and Caden and Lucas were twelve. Old enough to know Gwen and I weren't happily married, but too young to understand the dynamics of what went on. They understand now."

"And now? Does she want you back?"

Cam barked with laughter. The thought was absurd. "Fuck, no. And I sure as hell don't want to be wanted back. Gwen's happy with her life. I settled a decent amount on her when we divorced. Plus she inherited money from her mother a few years back. She doesn't need to work or anything. But when she gets bored, she likes to meddle."

"Meddle?"

"Meddle. Cause trouble. I'm guessing she heard about you and me in town. People saw us when I took you to dinner at the diner earlier this week and we were holding hands. Someone probably told her about it. She likes to be happy, but she's not as on board with my happiness. That's why she showed up today. She rarely comes to the ranch unless she needs to. I make sure she never needs to. So, are we good? Is there anything else you want to know?"

Noelle snuggled against his chest, and he breathed in her special scent, nuzzling her hair.

"We're good. I meant it when I said you didn't have to explain yourself. But I think she's crazy for ever letting you go."

Cam eased his body on top of hers, feeling the softness of her curves.

"We're better apart. Of course, she just might be crazy. I don't see her often anymore." Cam reached for the e-reader lying on the comforter. "What was my little sub reading? Something for your book club?"

Noelle turned a lovely shade of pink. She must be reading something really naughty.

"Just a book. But, yes, it's for the book club."

Cam eased his weight off of her and handed her the e-reader. "Read it to me."

She turned from pink to red. "I can't, Cam. I'd be too embarrassed."

Cam gave her his best Dom look and then used his best Dom voice.

"You know how to address me, little sub. This isn't a suggestion. Your Dom wants to hear your sweet voice reading."

Noelle's amber eyes grew wide, and her tongue snaked out to wet her lips. He felt the now-familiar tightening in his groin. She nodded.

"Yes, Sir. Should I start at the beginning?"

Cam shook his head and relaxed against the pillows. "No, just pick up where you left off. I love a good book before bed."

* * * *

Noelle's face was hot. It was times like this she cursed being a redhead. Her Dom knew she was incredibly embarrassed and he was enjoying it. He had a wicked smile playing around his well-shaped lips. She wanted to smack the top of his head with her e-reader. Such an action would get her flipped over his lap and her bottom sore and red. As it was, she had a punishment coming for dropping the F-word. A punishment she was probably going to enjoy. A lot.

He ran his hands around her generous breasts, plucking the nipples until they were hard and pointed. Before she could draw her next breath, a metal clamp was attached to her left nipple, and she cried out in surprise and pain. He watched, his face impassive, as she took deep breaths to deal with the bite on her tender flesh. When her breathing eased, he slowly pulled the other from his pocket and held it out with a smile.

He took his time, tweaking the nipple and then opening the cruel metal jaws of the clamp before her eyes. She tried not to tense up, but felt herself start to tremble as it moved closer. She sucked in a breath as the cold metal bit into sensitive skin. Her knees gave out, and she was now kneeling before him, a supplicant to her Master.

"Ah, that's where you belong, slave, at your Master's feet. Kiss them, sweet slave. Show me your submission."

She leaned forward, and the weights on the clamps pulled at her already sore nipples. She whimpered but pressed her lips to first one shiny, black boot, then the other.

Cam brushed her hard nipples, and she arched into the caress. Reading this to him was naughty and erotic, and she was flushed with arousal at the look of passion on his face.

"Would you like to be at my feet, sweet sub? I've never had a submissive kiss my feet, but the thought makes my cock hard as a rock."

She was breathing as hard as the submissive in the story.

"Yes, Sir. I think I would like to be at your feet." She grinned. "But I don't want to be accused of topping from the bottom."

Cam ran his fingers around the shadow of her rosy nipples through her shirt.

"Don't worry. Topping from the bottom will not be tolerated in any form. But there's never anything stopping you from kneeling at my feet. I don't have any rules against it. Continue, sub."

She kept her head down, waiting for his next command. It came in

*the form of his hand tugging at her hair. She pushed to her feet, but
kept her eyes down. She was not to look at him without his express
permission. She had already been punished once today.*

*He went to the cabinet, and she felt her heart race. The cabinet
held all manner of torture devices, and her Master's mind was
diabolical. She felt her pussy leak with her juices at what he might do
next.*

"Is that how it is, Noelle? Is it the unknown of what I might do
that makes you so aroused? So perfectly wet for me?"

His hand had trailed down her stomach, over her mound, and
burrowed into her pussy. He had a rule against panties, and she was
wet and ready for his questing fingers. He thrust one, then two fingers
into her cunt, and she moaned with the pleasure. If he would only rub
her clit, she knew she would go off like a rocket.

But, of course, he wasn't going to do that.

"Answer me, Noelle."

His voice was deep and dark, and she felt herself starting to go to
the place where the voices in her head were silent. She forced her
throat muscles to work.

"Yes, Sir. I love the way you keep me on the edge of not knowing.
I stay wet and ready for you, not because you have ordered me to be
ready for you at all times, but because I wonder what our next time
together will bring."

His fingers began a slow fucking rhythm, sending her halfway to
heaven, but no further.

"Read on, sub. You have all of my attention."

* * * *

Noelle's face was bright red, and her breathing was erratic. She
was highly aroused, and he was truly a sadistic bastard for making her
continue reading. But read on she would. Tonight he intended to teach

her about edging, and this was only the beginning.

He lifted her chin, bringing his lips to hers. His tongue sweeping her mouth, taking and demanding ownership. His hands were so hot, they were like branding irons on her body. She wanted to meld her body to his, become one with him. She reminded herself that her desires were not important. Her pleasure came from his desires.

He lifted his mouth from hers and smiled, running his finger down her body until his hand was poised next to a clamp. His eyes darkened, and then he gave the clamp a tug, sending pain and pleasure rushing through her body. The body that belonged to him.

"Do you like that, slave? Does it bring you pleasure? Perhaps this will bring you even more pleasure."

She shivered as he stepped back and showed her what he had retrieved from the cabinet. A leather flogger, its strands hanging down, looking innocuous to someone who didn't know how they felt against bare flesh. The thud of the heavy strands and the sting and heat left behind. She wanted to beg him to use her, and she wanted to beg him for mercy. She did neither, knowing she would acquiesce to his will.

Her last words were choked as he rubbed her G-spot. His hands were covered in her cream, and her pussy was clenched on his fingers. He could feel the flutters of an approaching orgasm. He pulled his hand out, sticky with her juices. She whimpered, her eyes dark with arousal, then finally begged from her full, lush lips.

"Please, Sir. Please, I need to come."

He shook his head. The night had only begun.

"No. It's not time yet. Lick my fingers clean."

He held his fingers in front of her lips and wondered if she would follow his command easily. Some women were squeamish about bodily fluids. She had swallowed his cum easily enough, but would she lick her own honey?

She hesitated for only a moment before her warm mouth and tongue began cleaning him. He waited patiently until she was done, his own cock hard and painful as she tortured him with her oral skills.

"I'm very pleased with you, Noelle. Tonight we're going to do something to push your boundaries. Do you know what edging is?"

Noelle shook her head. "No, Sir."

He ran his fingers through her fiery hair, letting the silken strands fall around her face.

"It's where the Dom, that's me, keeps the sub, that's you, on the edge of orgasm for an extended period of time. It makes the release exponentially more powerful when it happens. Sometimes too much pleasure can be painful. Not unbearably so. But uncomfortable. I want to take you out of your comfort zone tonight. I want to teach you about enduring something uncomfortable for your Dominant, for his pleasure. I want you to endure for me tonight."

He waited, watching her expression closely. This wasn't about pain. It was pure submission. She would let him keep her on the edge of climax until he, and only he, decided she should have her release. What she didn't know or realize yet was he would be uncomfortable, too. She would be torturing him as he was torturing her.

Her teeth bit into her soft lower lip before she nodded. "Yes, Sir. I will…endure for you."

He smiled and laid his hand on top of her head, accepting her submission. If it was possible, his cock hardened further, his balls hard and tight.

"Thank you, little sub. Tonight is not a test. This is simply another step in our journey together. You aren't being judged or graded. Do you understand, Noelle?"

"Yes, Sir."

"Then let's begin. Take off your shirt, lie back on the bed, and put your arms over your head."

Chapter Seven

What had she got herself into? Here she was lying back on the bed, sweetly submitting to what her loving Dom had pretty much admitted was going to be torture. For her, anyway. Right now, the promise of an explosive orgasm sometime later wasn't making her feel any braver.

I've lost my fucking mind.

He reached under the bed and pulled out a box. Somehow she knew the box was filled with the same thing the cabinet had been filled with in the book. Implements of pleasure and pain.

He pulled leather cuffs from the box and reached up and fastened them efficiently to her wrists, checking her circulation. She was surprised to find the cuffs were quite soft and cushioned. He then wrapped a strap around the thick beam in the middle of the headboard and attached it to each cuff. Now she knew why the bed looked like it was made from tree trunks. She was restrained to the headboard and could pull and tug all she wanted. The beam wasn't going to break, and the cuffs weren't going to give way. She pulled at the restraints, and they held fast.

Cam grinned. "Just had to test them, didn't you? Don't pull too hard. I don't want you bruised. The cuffs are padded, but they're not foolproof. You're very fair, and I'm guessing, from the spankings you've received, mark easily."

"I've never bruised."

"I know."

Warmth ran through her veins as she thought about how he took care of her. She hadn't had any marks because he made damn sure she didn't.

He reached for an ankle and stretched her wide, cuffing and attaching it to the footboard, then repeating the process on the other side. Finally, he tucked a cushion under her bottom. She was now spread wide, with her pussy pushed up and on display. She felt her honey trickling from her cunt and down her thighs. Being helpless like this was igniting her arousal like never before. She needed to come badly, but knew it wouldn't happen anytime soon.

He reached into the box and held up something fuzzy and blue, pressing it into her right hand.

"This is your safe word. Squeeze it."

She obediently squeezed the fluffy toy and it squeaked loudly, taking her by surprise.

"If at any time you simply cannot endure any longer, you squeeze the toy."

Noelle frowned in confusion as she stared at the squeaky toy. "Why can't I just tell you?"

"Because you'll be gagged."

Gagged?

"Um, I thought you said 'gagged,' Sir."

Cam laughed. "I did, pretty sub. I imagine you would get pretty loud with all the begging, moaning, whimpering, and of course, the screams when I finally let you come. We can't wake up the whole house. So you'll be gagged. It'll keep the noise level down. It'll also give you something to bite down on while I keep you on the edge."

"I guess I should say thank you, Sir."

"You're welcome. Now open wide."

He reached into the box again, pulling out something wrapped in plastic. He quickly pulled the plastic off and held it in front of her face.

"Open."

"It's a cock, Sir."

It was indeed a cock. A short, very fat cock. It was attached at the base to a plastic disc with straps on either side. He wanted to put that cock in her mouth.

"Yes, Noelle. It's a cock gag. It will keep your voice muffled and give you something to bite on. A ball gag isn't as comfortable. This also has a hole in the base so you can breathe through your mouth if you need to. Now, sub, don't make me say 'Open' a third time."

She heard the thread of steel running through his voice. How bad could having a cock in her mouth be? Especially one that was guaranteed not to come down her throat. She opened her lips, and he slipped the gag in, wrapping the straps around the back of her head and fastening the Velcro closure. It stretched her jaws wide and tasted a slightly acrid flavor from the plastic. There was no way to spit it out. It was staying until he decided to remove it or she squeezed the damn toy, one or the other. She panicked for a moment, and he immediately calmed her.

"Breathe, sweetheart. Take a deep breath. You can breathe through your mouth or nose. Everything is okay."

His voice was soothing, and she took several breaths, realizing what he said was true. She could easily breathe. She relaxed, and he smiled.

"Good girl. It's common to panic. Try to talk for me."

"Fmmlahun rheflmunh."

She sounded ridiculous, and no one would ever be able to make out a word, which was good because she'd called him a "fucking Dom." Perversely, the gag just made her hornier than ever. There was probably a puddle of cream underneath her pussy by now. He nodded in approval.

"Perfect. I love a gagged sub, honestly. So pretty. One more thing and then we'll get started."

He reached back into the box and out came a strip of black fabric. He held it up.

"A blindfold. It will make all your other senses come alive. I don't want you to panic. You have your safe word. Squeeze it for me, sweetheart."

She squeezed the toy. The squeak was annoying. He must have chosen this toy on purpose so she wouldn't just squeeze it for fun.

"Good girl. Let's get this blindfold on. Go ahead and close your eyes."

The dark fabric covered her eyes and wrapped around her head, fastening tightly. She was completely in the dark, not a sliver of light coming through anywhere. As he had predicted, her other senses became more acute. She could hear his breathing, and feel the crinkle of the hair on his arms next to hers. His fingers began caressing her breasts, plucking and tweaking the nipples. His mouth followed, and she arched her back, begging his lips and tongue to pleasure her more. Her nipples were hard, tight, and wet, and he blew his breath over the tips. She shivered in response, her entire body tuned to his. He kissed his way down her belly and back up her rib cage, nipping at the taut peaks quivering for his attention.

She was lulled into complacency when the metal clamp closed on her nipple. She had barely caught her breath when the other nipple was also clamped. She tried to twist her body and shake off the clamps, but they were fastened tight.

The pain shot straight to her clit and was now morphing to a dull ache. Each time she moved in the slightest, the clamps tugged at her sensitive nipples. She shouldn't like it, but she couldn't help herself. She could feel the dampness on the pillow underneath her. She had gushed even more honey from her needy pussy.

It felt like forever before he spoke.

"Good, sub. I'm going to leave those on for a while. In the meantime, let's take you right to the top."

She heard a humming and then felt the vibrator slip into her drenched cunt. She clenched on it, loving the feeling of being filled, finally. He began to fuck her with it very slowly, rubbing her G-spot with each stroke. She twisted and tried to urge him to move faster, but he wouldn't deviate from the slow, steady rhythm that was inexorably driving her crazy. As he had predicted, he was going to take her to the edge of orgasm but not let her go over. She moaned, but the gag muffled the sound. Her body was pulled taut, every muscle tight as she waited to go over.

The vibrator stopped. She protested, but he paid little heed to her muffled sounds. She felt the cold trickle of lubricant at her back hole, and something cold and plastic pressed against it. She tried to pull away and the clamps on her nipples tugged, sending more frissons of pleasure straight to her swollen clit.

"Do you need to use your safe word, Noelle?"

His hand stilled as he waited for her answer. She shook her head. This was submission, and she loved it. His fingers pressed the plastic into her backside insistently. She felt the stretching and a slight burn as her muscles gave way. She waited, wondering what he would do next. She almost came off the bed when the plug came alive in her ass.

Holy hell!

* * * *

Cam bit back his chuckle at Noelle's reaction to the vibrating plug in her ass. He was thrilled he would be the man to show her how pleasurable her body could be. All of her body.

She had reacted to the plug immediately, pulling even more at the restraints, twisting, and shuddering. She was so responsive, he would need to be careful she didn't climax without permission. He wasn't trying to set her up for any punishment. Tonight was purely about submission.

He petted her skin, and she moaned behind the gag. He skimmed a finger over her hard, swollen clit. She was very close to the edge. He powered down the butt plug and started the vibrator in her pussy. She began her climb again.

By the time he had repeated the vibrator, butt plug, vibrator pattern several times, she was flushed with arousal and begging to be finished. He couldn't make out her words, but the pleading tone was easy to make out. He couldn't leave her on the edge much longer.

He switched off both vibrators, pulled the large one from her slit, and leaned down to swipe his tongue through her folds, but avoiding direct contact with her clit. She tasted so sweet, he couldn't stop himself from eating at her sweet pussy, fucking her with his tongue. He could feel her cunt clench on his tongue, and one look at her right hand told him his sweet sub needed to come. Now. She was massaging the toy in her hand as if contemplating squeezing it.

He slid the vibrator back inside her, switched on both and plucked first one, then the other clamp off her nipples.

"Come now, sub."

He closed his mouth over her clit and sucked.

* * * *

Noelle was floating in some other reality. In this reality, she didn't worry or think about things. Feeling was all of her. Feeling was the only thing. And so much pleasure! Pleasure and pain were all mixed up, and the voices in her head were blissfully silent. She could hear her own voice in the distance. She was vaguely aware of her begging to be allowed to come, but the answer wasn't important. She only wanted to continue to feel this way forever.

Another sharp wave of pain jolted her, but the pleasure followed so quickly she must have been mistaken. She heard his voice, and she couldn't stop herself from falling over the cliff. She soared in freedom. She heard her voice again, but this time it wasn't pleading. It was jubilant. Every part of her burst open, and the pleasure poured from her. It seemed to go on forever, and then it finally ebbed, leaving her wrung out and weak, but somehow content.

When she opened her eyes, she was untied, the gag and blindfold tossed on the nightstand. Cam was cuddling her close, whispering words of praise. She struggled to sit up, pushing at his arms.

"Relax, little sub. You've been in subspace for some time. Let yourself come down slowly."

She frowned, trying to put the puzzle of the last few minutes together.

"I…um…What happened? How did I get untied?"

Cam rubbed her back and shoulders. "I untied you, Noelle. I also pulled the gag out and took the blindfold off. You were in subspace. Your mind shut off while you were feeling something so intense. It took a few minutes for it turn back on, that's all. Everything is okay. I promise you. I will always take care of you. Just relax and let yourself drift to earth. This is our time together for me to show you how incredible you are."

Noelle lay back on his chest, listening to his steady heartbeat. She had read about subspace but hadn't expected to experience it herself. She was too much of a control freak. She understood now why he had wanted to take her to the edge for so long. It took her that long to let go of the control.

"I'm okay. I just feel a little…freaky. It's weird to lose a few minutes of your life."

He tilted her chin up so her eyes met his. The tenderness and emotion she saw almost took her breath away.

"You're the most amazing woman I have ever met, Noelle. I've never received such sweet submission in my life. I'm humbled. I'm not even sure how to react."

He reached for a bottle of water next to the bed, urging her to drink. She was thirsty and drained half the bottle easily.

"Good girl. Are you hungry?"

Cam eased from her arms, but she shook her head and pulled him back down. This snuggling afterward felt great. She'd never dated a man who liked to cuddle as much as Cam.

She ran her finger down his chest, feeling very bold all of a sudden.

"Sir made me feel awesome. How may I now serve, Sir?"

Cam quirked an eyebrow.

"I have one or two ideas. Are you sure you're ready?"

Noelle giggled. "I was born ready, Sir."

* * * *

His beautiful submissive was going to be the death of him. Her submission had practically brought him to his knees. He had never been given so much trust from a woman. Her ability to give astounded him. He wanted to fill her with more pleasure than she had ever known, knowing it would flow back to him. She was a giver. He would have to make sure she took pleasure, too. She was certainly well on her way to taking his heart.

She was leaning back on the pillow, looking very satisfied. Her skin glowed from her orgasm, and her eyes sparkled with mischief. He got on his knees and placed a leg on each side of her, holding his aching cock in front of her face. There wasn't any doubt what he wanted. He wanted her sweet lips on his cock, and he wanted it now.

She licked her lips and opened her mouth with a smile. He leaned forward, bracing himself on the headboard, the tip of his cock running along her lips. Her tongue snaked out and took a taste of him, and he groaned. The sensations ran along his length and straight to his balls. Her torture had been his torture, and he was ready to shoot his load.

Her hot, wet mouth engulfed the head, and his hand automatically went to the back of her head, his fingers tangling in her hair. She took up a rhythm that was destined to send him over the edge within minutes, but he pulled away, his cock making a pop sound as it emerged, shiny from her oral ministrations. His little slave pouted, her lower lip swollen.

"I didn't finish pleasuring you, Sir."

"I know, pretty sub. As much as I love your warm mouth, I want to fuck your hot pussy."

He reached down and grabbed her legs, pulling her flat on her back and spreading her pussy wide. He wanted her to come again, and he needed to get her juices flowing.

"Hold yourself wide for me. I want something hot to eat."

Noelle's face, neck, and chest flushed with her arousal. She loved to have her pussy licked. He pressed his face to her mound and breathed deeply. He loved her sweet, musky smell. The red curls tickled his nose, and he had a wicked thought. He tugged at the crinkly hair covering her pussy.

"Submissives usually have bare cunts. I'm going to shave this pussy."

Noelle dropped her legs, her eyes wide. "Now? Are you crazy?"

Before she could react, he rolled her over and deposited six smacks hard to her bottom cheeks, his hand making lovely pink marks on the pale skin.

"That's 'Now, *Sir*? Are you crazy, *Sir*?' Get back into position while I get the supplies."

"Sorry, Sir." He rolled her onto her back and gave her a stern look, and her top teeth sunk into her swollen bottom lip. She knew better than to act like that.

He bounded into the bathroom, grabbing what he needed, and took a peek into the bedroom. She was lying with her legs spread as instructed. He threw the towel over his shoulder and strolled back into the room. She looked apprehensive about what was about to happen.

Good.

A sub should be kept off-balance from time to time. No Dom wanted to be completely predictable. What a bore.

"Keep those legs spread and stay very still. I don't want to nick anything."

If anything, her amber eyes went even wider, and she froze into position. He placed a towel underneath her, then reached for the scissors to trim the hair short. She didn't have a lot of curls, but they would be easier to shave if they were trimmed close.

He clipped each curl and let it fall on the towel. When he was done, he placed the hot towel on her cunt, and she jumped at the heat.

"Easy, Noelle. Does it burn?"

Noelle shook her head. "No, Sir. I just wasn't expecting it."

He pulled the towel off and shook the shaving gel can, spraying a generous amount. He picked up the new razor and began at the top of her mound, rinsing the blades in the bowl of hot water he had filled in the bathroom. She was holding still, and he moved down, closer to her clit. Each flick of the razor seemed to send her arousal higher. She was leaking cream on the towel, and her clit was swelling out of its hood.

He placed his hand on her stomach to keep her from moving.

"I'm going to do around your clit and your pussy lips. Stay perfectly still, Noelle."

Her breathing was becoming shallower, and her nipples were peaked. She was enjoying this. He drew it out longer than it needed to be. Each stroke of the blades, baring her delicate, pink skin. By the time he was done, her cunt was drenched, and she looked primed and ready to fuck. He quickly rinsed her, rubbing some lotion into the skin. She was moaning and panting as he drew circles around her clit.

"Oh God, please fuck me, Sir!"

He slipped a finger inside, her pussy sucking his finger in. He rubbed her G-spot and leaned down to torture her with featherlight licks on her pussy. Her back was arched, and her head was thrashing back and forth as he used his tongue up and down, back and forth over that shiny pearl until she was on the brink of climax.

He grabbed a condom from the nightstand and suited up. He wouldn't last long in her hot, tight cunt. He thrust all the way to his balls and groaned at the perfection. He gritted his teeth, before pulling out and slamming back in. He rode her fast and hard, loving the way she responded to his every stroke and touch. Her unrestrained hands were raking her nails down his back, and her pelvis was meeting his every thrust. She loved fucking as much as he did, and she sure as hell wasn't ashamed to show it.

She ground her clit against his groin, and he knew she was about to go over. He whispered filthy, dirty words to urge her on, finally letting himself go when he felt her convulse around him. Her pussy clamped down, and his balls drew up, the pressure in his lower back becoming too much. He stiffened as the pleasure slammed into him over and over again. His hot seed filled the condom, and he shuddered as he came back down to earth, collapsing on top of Noelle, sweaty and sated.

He gave her a slow, wet kiss before rolling off and pulling her to his side. She fit like she had been made to sleep there. He disposed of the condom in the trash and pulled her closer, listening to their breathing and their heartbeats synchronize. Noelle was already asleep, her face relaxed and angelic with the moonlight streaming in the room from the window. Cam stayed awake for quite a while longer, stroking her hair and wondering what the future would bring for both of them.

Chapter Eight

"Cam, stop fussing. I know how to ride."

She earned herself a hard look from Cam that promised retribution. Abby and Noelle had decided to go for a horseback ride since the weather was starting to warm up, and Cam and Brody were saddling a couple of horses for them. The way Cam was acting, he must think she didn't have a lick of sense. He'd been lecturing her for the last ten minutes.

"I'm not fussing, and dammit, Noelle, listen to me. This ranch isn't a kiddie park, and these horses aren't from a petting zoo. It's dangerous out there. Now promise me right now that you and Abby will be back in a couple of hours. It's too dangerous to be caught out when it starts to get dark, plus the weather has been unpredictable this spring. Promise me."

Noelle sighed. "Cross my heart and hope to die. I promise."

Cam's lips tightened. She was pissing him off royally. *Oh goody.*

One glance at Brody's wide grin, and she knew they were putting on a show. Cam was ribbed unmercifully by his sons and brother for being such a hard-ass. He wasn't going to let this little rebellion of disrespect go unnoticed and unpunished.

"Sounds sincere to me, Dad." Amusement laced Brody's tone.

Cam never looked up from Noelle. "Stay out of this, son. Don't you have your own woman to worry about?"

"My woman is perfectly trained."

Abby chose that moment to blow a raspberry. Noelle cracked up, but almost choked in surprise as Brody tossed Abby over his knee and proceeded to spank her bottom hard. Abby was yelping and giggling, so there was probably no real pain involved, especially since she was wearing thick blue jeans as protection. Noelle eyed Cam, hoping she wasn't next. She sighed when he pointed to the tack room.

"March, sub. Now."

He had turned into her mean Dom, and she headed for the tack room knowing she was about to get a warm bottom. She shrugged. She was going to be sore from riding anyway.

He followed her closely and closed the door behind them.

"I'm not a fan of public punishments. You and Abby are being deliberately defiant. I can't let this pass. Pull your jeans and panties down."

Noelle stood there for a moment. Cam's expression brooked no defiance, and his body language told her he wasn't kidding. She was in trouble. She dropped her eyes and quickly unfastened her jeans, pushing them and her panties down to midthigh. She waited as he circled her, finally coming up behind her and turning her so she faced a wooden table. He pressed on her back until her hands came down on the surface.

"You can brace yourself here. Six for your very deliberate defiance."

She felt the cool air caress her bare bottom and sucked in a breath. She loved his spankings, and today would be no exception. Already, she was starting to trickle honey from her pussy. The thought of his hand coming down on her ass had her arousal in a tizzy. She couldn't stop her wriggle of excitement.

The waiting seemed to take forever as she stood there, bent over, legs spread, her ass on display and the perfect target. Finally, he took pity on her and administered the first stroke. The whack of his hand sent her up on her toes and fire straight to her pussy. He let the heat from the first stroke simmer before the second. It didn't add to the pain, just heightened the heat. She thrust her bottom out for more and was gratified when he gave it to her. Four more strokes were applied to her ass cheeks, multiplying the heat in her pussy. She was dripping cream down her thighs when he finished. His hand rubbed her hot cheeks and slipped between her legs, finding her extremely drenched pussy.

"Pull your pants up, sub. We're done."

She pulled her jeans up and refastened them. Her ass cheeks were on fire, and it was going to be an uncomfortable ride. She gave him her best regretful look.

"I'm sorry, Sir."

He sighed. "I'm sorry, too, Noelle. I'm protective because I know the things that can happen on a ranch. I don't want anything to happen to you. Ever."

He pulled her close, his hands massaging her sore bottom.

"Just once I'd like to give you a spanking that you don't enjoy. Next time, little sub, I use my belt." He pulled back and gave her a stern look. "So let's not have a next time."

"Yes, Sir," Noelle said as meekly as she could manage. She'd tell him later how much she wanted to be spanked by his belt. She hoped it would be his spanking implement of choice in the future.

"May we kiss and make up, Sir?"

His face relaxed. "Yes, my gorgeous but naughty sub, we can kiss and make up. I know I'm a strict Dom. I guess I'm lucky you like the punishments."

She giggled, her lips tasting a trail across his square jaw. "Then it won't come as a surprise that I want to be spanked by your belt? I was going to tell you later tonight, but I'll just tell you now. I'm as horny as the devil, Cam, just thinking about it."

She felt his chuckle as he nuzzled her neck.

"You'll have to wait until later, baby. The big, bad Dom has work to do. Be a good girl, okay?"

She nodded as his lips came down on hers, sending her world into a spin. She was already looking forward to later.

* * * *

Noelle breathed deeply. The spring air in Montana was so sweet. So different than the salty air in Florida. The valley was beautiful, tucked in between mountain ranges. The sky looked the same blue as Cam's eyes when he was making love.

Cam.

She had been at the ranch two weeks now. She was falling harder and harder for him, and he seemed to return her feelings. She couldn't doubt his commitment to their relationship. He was slowly and patiently teaching her about submission. Heaven knew she had a long way to go to be his perfect sub. She'd earned a myriad of punishments since agreeing to be his sub. The spanking earlier had only been one of them. She squirmed on her saddle. Her bottom was still a little sore.

"Is your ass as sore as mine?"

Abby was rubbing her bottom with her hand ruefully. Noelle laughed.

"A little. It was going to be sore anyway, so I guess it isn't a big deal. I didn't think you would be sore. You're wearing jeans. I got mine bare bottom, thank you very much."

Abby's eyed went wide. "Brody was pretty mad when I blew that raspberry. Bare bottom, huh? Does Cam keep paddles in the barn for punishment?"

Noelle knew Cam had a reputation for being a strict, mean Dom. Abby probably thought Cam had blistered her bottom.

"Well, he might. He used his hand today. It was hot, but too quick. I hope he does it again."

Abby laughed. "Oh, I love a good, hard spanking. Wow, you have Cam wrapped around your finger. I would have thought you wouldn't be able to walk straight after one of his punishments. You breezed out of the tack room with a blush and a smile."

"Cam's punishments are pretty mild, little sister. Um, have you talked to Brody about our family yet? I mean they can't go around spanking and ordering us around in front of our parents. They're way too uptight for that."

Abby groaned. "I did. He said they knew how to act around company. I'm not looking forward to Mom and Dad being here. I can only imagine how they are going to react to my living here after we're married."

Noelle frowned. "You're already living here. Don't tell me Mom and Dad don't know you're going to be living here from now on?"

Abby chewed her bottom lip. "I'm not like you, Elle. You're strong and independent. I get around our parents and wilt. When they call, they've been pressuring me to get Brody to move to Florida after we're married."

Noelle threw up her hands. "And do what?"

Abby ran her hand over her face and grimaced. "They want him to go to law school."

Noelle barked with laughter. "What is this obsession with a lawyer in the family? Are they planning to knock over a bank or something?"

Abby sputtered with laughter. "That would be funny. Our uptight parents in prison orange."

Noelle was laughing with Abby when they heard it. It sounded like gunshots not very far away. She didn't have time to react before her horse was rearing up in fear. Noelle held on for dear life, but her feet dislodged from the stirrups, and she fell to the ground with a sickening thud, jarring every bone in her body and probably loosening a few teeth. She hadn't let go of the reins when her horse took off like a shot, dragging her several yards over the rough, rocky ground before she could untangle her fingers.

"Elle! Elle! Oh dear God, Elle! Are you all right? Can you talk?"

Noelle tried to move, but Abby kept her still.

"Don't move. You may have hurt yourself."

Her choking laughter hurt. "I can guarantee you, sis, I've hurt myself. Shit, my head hurts."

She reached up and felt a goose egg on her forehead. When she brought her hand down, it was smeared with blood. She gingerly moved her limbs, wincing when she tried to move her right ankle and left wrist.

"Stay there. I'll call the men on the satellite phone Brody put in my pack."

Noelle stared up at the blue sky, every part of her body starting to ache.

"I don't think I could move if I wanted to. What happened to Turismo?"

"The horse took off and is probably halfway to the ranch by now. Elle, you're not going to pass out on me, are you? You need to stay awake. You may have a concussion."

Noelle's lids felt very heavy. "I'm just closing them against the sun."

She heard Abby's voice on the phone and her reassuring hand on her forehead.

"Stay with me, Elle. Cam and Brody are on their way."

"Great. Cam gets to tell me how right he was. I'm never going to hear the end of this."

Abby patted her hand. "Neither will I, sis. Neither will I."

* * * *

The next twenty-four hours passed in a blur. Cam, Colt, Brody, Caden, and Lucas had all shown up. Cam looked grim-faced and didn't say much, but held her tenderly in the backseat of the Land Rover all the way to the hospital in Bozeman. He had stayed by her side in the emergency room until the intimidating nurse had shooed him away. Even then, he had growled his frustration and promised to be back as soon as he could.

He had kept his promise, holding her hand and talking softly to her when she had been safely ensconced into a hospital bed for the night. They said it was for observation. It appeared to be for driving her Dom and man insane. He was beside himself with worry, and nothing she said to the contrary seemed to make him any calmer. She hadn't minded when the dragon-lady nurse kicked him out for the night so she could get some rest.

Now it was the next day, and she was tucked up into Cam's bed at the ranch with her right ankle wrapped up and propped on a pillow. Her left wrist was also wrapped up, and her body was covered in bruises and scrapes. There was a bandage on her forehead, and she had a lovely shiner on her right eye. She was truly a vision to behold. If she was trying for pity sex, she was certainly on the right track. Cam would have to be downright crazy to want her in this condition.

Which was a shame, since all she had to do was doze and read her naughty, smutty books. All she could think about was jumping her man's sexy-as-sin body. "How are you feeling, sweetheart?"

Cam stood at the door with a tray of food and a tentative smile. She threw her e-reader down on the bed next to her and waved him in.

"Pretty strange, actually. These painkillers are doing funny things to my brain."

He set the tray down on the bed and helped her sit up, fluffing the pillows behind her.

"It's nice to have a slave of my own. Do you do windows, too?"

She giggled, realizing the pills were making her say crazy things. Cam gave her an indulgent smile.

"I'm just taking care of you, precious. You scared the bejesus out of me and everyone, falling off Turismo like that. I want you to get better. We have your birthday party coming up."

Cam was throwing a big barn dance for her thirtieth birthday.

"Maybe we should make it a costume party. I can go as Quasimodo."

Cam frowned. "You look fine."

"No, I don't. I look like I went ten rounds with Chuck Norris."

Cam fussed, placing the napkin on her lap and pulling the plastic wrap off the piping-hot food. Noelle brushed his hands away.

"Go ahead and say it. I know you're dying to. Let's just get it over with."

His mouth twisted. "What am I dying to say?"

"That you were right and I was wrong. Ranches are dangerous places, and I ended up getting hurt. You had to take me to the hospital, and now you have to take care of the invalid."

The medication was really messing with her. She was now so bored she was trying to pick a fight.

Cam's eyes narrowed, and he took a deep breath. "Sweetheart, if you are trying to say I'm happy you got hurt or I resent taking care of you, you couldn't be further from the truth. I'm very sorry you got hurt. Turismo shouldn't have reared up like that. None of this is your fault. It was an accident, pure and simple. Yes, accidents happen on ranches, and that's why you need to be careful. But this was nothing anyone could have foreseen."

"So you aren't mad?"

"No, I am not mad. And I like taking care of you, by the way. I don't like you to be hurt, but I do like spoiling and coddling you. Although, on those pills you certainly don't act like your usual self. You're sweet and submissive one minute and meaner than a rattler the next. I hope there are no refills on that prescription."

Noelle rolled her eyes. She knew she was an emotional roller coaster right now, but he didn't need to remind her. Perhaps changing the subject was a good idea.

"Is Turismo okay? You won't shoot him or anything, will you?"

"Of course not. We will do some more training with him, so he won't be so jumpy next time. Luckily, Abby's horse was much older and slower and didn't react to the sound. It would have been much worse if you both were hurt."

Noelle picked at her food. "Did you find out what made the noise? I swear it sounded like gunshots, Cam. I've heard gunfire when I lived in New York."

A muscle worked in Cam's jaw. "No, we didn't. I can't for the life of me imagine who would be out there shooting a gun. But when I find out—"

She caressed his arm, trying to soothe him. "Relax, my mean Dom. You've been wound tighter than a drum since yesterday. I'm okay. I was lucky. I landed on my hard head."

That got a smile from him. He raised her hand to his lips and kissed it, frowning at the bruises and scrapes from the twisted reins.

"And your back and bottom, too, sub. Why don't you finish dinner and I'll come up and help you into the bathtub. It's got a Jacuzzi setting, and it might help all those sore muscles."

Noelle smiled and lifted a spoonful of potatoes to her mouth. "Now that finally sounds like a plan. Me naked and you running your hands all over me."

Cam laughed as he headed out of the bedroom. "No way, baby. This is going to be a chaste bathing. You're in no condition to be seducing me."

Her pillow hit the door just as he closed it, his laughter trailing down the hall. Her Dom was an evil man. She was just going to have to convince him she was feeling fine.

* * * *

Cam slumped on the kitchen counter, sipping at his coffee. It tore his guts up to see his woman hurting. He knew she was in pain and the marks on her body made him mad as hell. Just what had spooked Turismo? He'd talked to all the hands, and none of them admitted to firing a gun yesterday.

Guns were a fact of life on a working ranch. All the groups carried a rifle in case they came across the odd snake or coyote. But something told Cam this wasn't an accident. He straightened up as Colt came into the kitchen. He didn't look any happier than Cam felt.

"Well, what's the verdict?"

Colt pulled a mug from the cupboard and poured himself some coffee.

"I asked around. Gwen was seen at a charity event for the hospital yesterday afternoon. It couldn't have been her trying to scare the horse."

Cam exhaled slowly. "Then who, Colt? No one should have even been in the vicinity of where Abby and Noelle were riding, let alone shooting a gun."

Colt lowered himself into a kitchen chair with a grunt. "Listen, Gwen's crazy. I'll give you that. I wouldn't put it past her to want to hurt anyone or anything that made you happy. But you know as well as I do, Gwen hates guns. She wouldn't touch one when she lived here at the ranch. She didn't do this."

"I know. But Gwen has a cruel streak a mile wide as you well know. This would be something she'd do. God knows she tried to mess with your relationship with Julie."

Gwen had tried to come between Colt and his wife by putting doubts about Colt's fidelity in Julie's mind and throwing herself at Colt. It had been just one of the many mind games Gwen had played when they were married.

Colt's expression grew hard. He didn't have any patience for Gwen's crap. "She'll never do that again. Your punishment for her behavior was extremely effective."

Cam had forbidden her to go to the club for several months. Gwen had bitched and fumed the entire time, but he hadn't backed down. Taking away her means to get the pain she craved had been his only weapon to combat her continual bad behavior.

"So now what? If it's not Gwen, are we saying it was an accident?"

Colt nodded. "For now, I think we have to think it's possible it was an accident. Maybe one of the hands was using a gun and is afraid to admit it. Shit, Cam, you have to admit you were pretty intense when you questioned them. They were all scared as fuck for their jobs."

"Hell, I just wanted a fucking answer."

Cam glanced at the clock. "Noelle should be done with dinner. I'm going to help her take a bath."

Colt snorted. "Help? Is that some kind of euphemism?"

"She's hurt, bro. I don't think she's in any shape for a scene with her Dom, for fuck's sake."

"Yeah, she's going to look up at you with those golden-brown eyes and her soft, naked skin, and you're going to be a fucking angel. Don't let your halo fall down and strangle you, big brother."

"I can be an angel."

Colt slapped him on the back and grinned. "Sure you can. A fallen angel. Take good care of your woman and think pure thoughts."

Cam walked up the stairs with a grimace. He hadn't had a pure thought since meeting Noelle.

* * * *

Noelle steadied herself as she stood up from the bed she'd been occupying for the last several hours. Cam was in the bathroom running her a hot bath, and she was thoroughly sick and tired of doing nothing. She didn't want to take any more pain pills, either. They were messing with her head and making things fuzzy.

She limped across the room, wincing at the soreness in her limbs. Every inch of her ached, and this soak in the tub was going to feel heavenly. She had almost made it across the room when Cam came out of the bathroom and immediately scowled.

"I told you I would carry you. You could fall and hurt yourself."

He crossed the room in seconds and scooped her up in his arms.

"I'm already hurt, Cam. The only way I could hurt myself more is if I took a flying leap from the bedroom window. I'm sick of lying in bed. I just wanted to stretch my legs. You don't want me to get a blood clot, do you?"

He dropped her on the bathroom vanity, and the V between his brows became even more pronounced.

"Of course I don't want you to get a blood clot. I'm trying to look after you, dammit."

Noelle had to hide her laughter. He really was cute in this mood.

"I know you are, and you're doing a great job. Dinner was great. But I can't lie in bed forever. Even with a man as sexy as you are."

She trailed her hands down his chest, heading straight for his cock. She was pretty sure he wouldn't punish her for touching him without permission when she was in this shape. He caught her hands and rolled his eyes.

"No way, Noelle. Practically every inch of your body is covered in bruises. We're not having sex."

She looked at his erection pressing against his zipper.

"Are you sure? Little Cam doesn't look convinced."

He started pulling her T-shirt over her head.

"Using the word 'little' anywhere in the vicinity of my cock isn't going to get you laid, pretty sub."

Laughter bubbled up. "Your cock is huge, and you damn well know it. I'm just asking you to use it, that's all."

Cam tossed the T-shirt on the floor and unwrapped her ankle and wrist, before lowering her gently into the swirling water. She sighed in contentment as the hot water soothed her aches and pains.

"No."

"No? Just 'no'?"

"You want a complete sentence? Okay. No, I am not using my cock. No. And don't say 'damn.' I'll catalog that offense for a future punishment."

Noelle crossed her arms over her breasts and pouted. "You're mean."

Cam started washing her long hair, and it was hard to stay cranky when his strong fingers were kneading her scalp. He was careful to stay away from her bandaged forehead.

"Yep, that's me. One mean-assed Dom. I'm not sure why you put up with me, frankly. Lean back so I can rinse your hair."

She closed her eyes and let herself relax. She knew he would take the utmost care with her.

"You're a wonderful man, Cam. The best I've ever known. Frankly, that's why I put up with you."

His hands paused and then she felt his lips against hers, very softly. She raised her arms and wound them around his neck, starved for his kiss. She didn't want to go another twenty-four hours without his masterful touch ever again. The kiss seemed to go on forever, their tongues playing tag and sending arousal sizzling through her veins. She forgot all about her bruises and scrapes, letting the world slip away to just her man and how he made her feel. She whimpered when he lifted his mouth from hers.

"You're gonna be the death of me, sweetheart. But damn, it's a hell of a way to go. I can't deny you anything."

He leaned over and captured a nipple in his mouth, running his tongue around it and scraping it lightly with his teeth. She tried to arch her back, but he held her down firmly so she wouldn't jar her sore body. His mouth was sending sparks of pleasure straight to her cunt. It had been too long since she'd felt his cock driving them both to the heights of passion.

"Please, Sir."

Her voice sounded breathless and needy. His hand skimmed down her belly and parted her folds to stroke her sensitive flesh. Heat suffused her entire body, and she grabbed his arm to stop the dizzy sensation that had nothing to do with her medication, and everything to do with how he could make her feel.

"I'll take care of you, sweetheart. Just lie still and let me do the work."

His mouth captured her other nipple as his fingers found her swollen clit. She was so turned-on it only took him seconds to bring her to climax. He held her tenderly as her body shook and waves of pleasure ran through her, making sure she didn't further injure herself. She slumped in the water as the final wave ebbed away. She reached for Cam and ran a hand down his chest.

"I can't feel any pain. You washed it all away."

Cam's jaw was tight. "Endorphins. They'll wear off eventually. Let's get you dressed and in bed before they do."

He lifted her from the tub and set her on her feet, uncaring that he was getting soaked in the process. She looked down and his cock was clearly outlined in his jeans. He had to be in pain.

"Please, Sir. May I bring you pleasure, too?"

Cam swung away to grab a towel. "No. You're hurt."

"But I—"

Cam lifted her chin to stare into his blue eyes. "I said no. Stop topping from the bottom. I mean it, Noelle. I am in charge in this bedroom, and I have a long memory for transgressions. I'll add this to your ever-growing list for punishment at a later date."

Noelle bit her lip. "I'm sorry, Sir."

His started drying her legs with a towel. "Thank you, Noelle." He looked up at her, his face softening. "And thank you for caring. It's not something I'm used to."

She gave him a saucy smile. "Best get used to it, Sir. I'm going to drive you crazy and get hundreds of spankings."

He swung her up in his arms and carried her to the bed.

"I'm a lucky Dom."

She shook her head. "No, you're a lucky man."

Chapter Nine

The short scruff of his beard teased the inside of her quivering thighs as he kissed his way up her body. She wanted to beg for his tongue, but couldn't bring herself to utter the words. She'd wanted him for so long and still couldn't believe he was really here with her. She kept thinking he would disappear and she would be alone with her vibrator like so many other lonely nights. He seemed to sense her disquiet and ran a soothing hand up her thigh.

"I'm going to fuck you until you can't walk or remember your own name. The only thing you'll remember is my name, and you'll scream it over and over when you find your release."

His arrogant words brought her out of her reverie. She gave him a challenging smile and spread her legs wide.

"Bring it on, cowboy. Fuck me like you mean it."

He brushed her pussy lips with his hard cock.

"Make no mistake, Gisella. I mean it."

Then he thrust into her all the way to his balls, sending pleasure shooting through her body. She couldn't stop herself crying out his name.

He gave her an evil smile. "That's right. Scream my name, witch."

Tori smiled wistfully. "I want to be fucked until I can't walk or remember my own name. I'm jealous." She looked at the other women hopefully. "Please tell me it's not all it's cracked up to be."

The other women looked at each other dubiously. Finally, Lisa pointed to the camera where Noelle was attending via Skype.

"I, personally, think it is, but maybe Noelle can say it's not."

Noelle thought about her mean Dom and their naughty sex play. He hadn't fucked her since her riding accident, and it was driving her crazy. She was practically good as new, and still he held back. She was ready to find his toys and tie him to the bed for her own pleasure.

"Sorry, Tori. It's freakin' awesome. You need to find yourself a man."

Sara giggled. "Or two."

Brianne rolled her eyes and sipped her cosmo. "Most people don't find two men who are willing to share one woman. You won the lottery, my dear."

Sara sighed, a blissful look on her face. "I know. Jeremy and Cole are the world's best lovers."

Noelle shook her head. "Cam is the best lover. Hands down."

Lisa arched her perfectly shaped eyebrows. "I'd argue for Conor, and I'm sure Brianne would argue for Nate, but I want to hear more from you. Seems like you and Cam have gotten very close. Is it love?"

Noelle was silent for a moment as her time with Cam rushed through her mind. The laughter, the fun, the lovemaking were out of this world. "Yes. It's love. I love him. Shit, I haven't even told Cam yet. I've barely admitted it to myself until now. But, fuck it all, I love him. How could I not fall in love with him? He's everything I've been looking for in a man, but could never find. He's honest, hardworking, respectful, he likes kids and dogs, he's caring and gentle, yet knows when to take control. He's handsome as sin and amazing in bed. He's everything."

Brianne grinned. "Elle, you have no idea how happy we are for you. We've been hoping you would find someone who made you feel this way. Isn't finding the right man wonderful?"

Brianne had been euphoric since falling in love with Dr. Nate Hart, but she had always had a romantic streak in her.

"Yes, but I need to think practically right now."

Sara popped a truffle in her mouth. "Practically? What about?"

"Does he love me, too? I think he does, but he's never said it. Also, we live, what, twenty states apart? I can't ask him to leave the ranch. It's not only his livelihood, it's his family home. I'd have to move to Montana. It snows in Montana. I remember snow in New York. It's cold and wet."

Tori laughed. "You'll have your love and very hot sex to keep you warm on those long winter nights."

Sara leaned into the camera. "If you love each other, you'll work it out. Look at me and the boys. You're self-employed, and technically you could work anywhere you wanted to. Do you want to be with him?"

Noelle nodded. "Hell, yes."

Lisa raised her martini glass. "Then go all out and do it. Hell, we know you're not afraid to take chances. Don't be a pussy now when it really counts."

Noelle raised her glass in agreement. "Got it. No being a pussy allowed. I'm going after what I want. Starting tomorrow night."

Brianne smiled. "What's tomorrow night?"

"My thirtieth birthday party, that's what. I'll show Cam my appreciation for throwing me a birthday party in my own inimitable style. In other words, I'm gonna rock his world!"

The women laughed until Lisa cleared her throat. "Speaking of birthdays…You should be getting a little birthday care package from us tomorrow. Enjoy it. And we'll want details next week."

Noelle shook her head, laughing at Lisa's mysterious smile.

"I'm truly scared of what you all have wrapped up and mailed to me. I hope it's not flammable."

Lisa frowned and turned to Tori. "It's not flammable, is it?"

Tori put her finger over her lips. "You're going to ruin the surprise."

Noelle groaned. She now knew to open the box in private. Heaven only knew what her crazy girlfriends had sent her. But she had to admit, finding out would be fun.

* * * *

Noelle was walking slowly across the barn, looking luscious in tight blue jeans and a white silk blouse. Her long hair was loose and wavy around her shoulders, and her lips were shiny and kissable. His cock immediately stood up and took notice, pressing against his button fly insistently.

Down boy. The night's just begun.

Cam had plans tonight for his sweet submissive. The wedding was only a few weeks away, and Cam only had this short time to prove to her they belonged together. Even if she decided to go back to Florida, he wanted this birthday to be the most memorable of her life.

"Happy Birthday, sweetheart. Have you had a good day so far?"

He pulled her close, letting her scent envelope him.

"You would know, cowboy. I believe I had a handsome seminaked man bring me breakfast in bed this morning. The only downside was that he wasn't completely naked. I've been thinking about him all day."

Cam wound a silky strand of her hair around his fingers. "Who is this guy? Is he any competition?"

Noelle giggled, and he felt his heart tighten in his chest. He had fallen for this red-haired temptress.

"He's everything to me. I'm completely crazy about him."

Cam shook his head. "Always the luck. The lady is taken."

Noelle let her hands wander down his back to cup his ass through his jeans.

"Actually, the lady hasn't been *taken* in about a week. She's starting to think he doesn't want her."

"Trust me. He does. He's going to prove it tonight."

He felt her shiver and nuzzled her neck, nibbling on the soft, fragrant skin. She pulled back and held out a package for him.

"It's not my birthday, sweetheart."

She rolled her eyes. "Tell that to my friends in Florida. I'm supposed to give this to you. They sent me a birthday care package today."

He eyed the package suspiciously, especially as Noelle's fair skin began to get pink with embarrassment. He separated the envelope from the box and pulled out the letter.

Dear Noelle's Dom,

We want Noelle to have a wonderful birthday, so we have enclosed a fun item. We hope you enjoy it, too. This should be under your control now. Please do not think we are trying to top from the bottom, as our husbands have devious ways of punishing us.

Respectfully,

Lisa, Brianne, Tori, and Sara

P.S. If you break her heart, we don't care if you're a Dom or not. We'll come out to Montana and kick your ass.

Cam chuckled as he glanced at Noelle's fiery red cheeks.

"Do you know what's in here, little sub?"

She nodded. "Not for sure, but I have a pretty good idea."

He opened the box and pulled out a flat silver square with multiple buttons. He frowned and pressed one at random. Noelle jumped as if he had touched her with a cattle prod. She grabbed his arm and closed her eyes, licking her lips. She was starting to become aroused.

* * * *

Don't antagonize the mean Dom.

Somehow, she couldn't stop herself. She loved to poke at his dominant personality and see how he would respond. Now he had that fucking evil remote, and she might as well give him a good reason to torture her, since she was sure he would find a reason no matter what.

The butterfly was resting directly on her clit and sending vibrations up it, straight to her weeping cunt. Her panties were soaked, and she was ready for an orgasm. One look at Cam's expression told her it would be a while in coming. He was amused by her defiance, but as intractable as a stone wall in dealing with it. A month ago she would have laughed if anyone had told her she would have fallen in love with a strict, no-nonsense Dom. But here she was, head over heels for Cam Hunter and loving it. No wonder she'd never found the right man before. She'd been looking in all the wrong places.

The vibrations stopped as abruptly as they started. She let her body relax slightly, but not all the way, on guard in case it started again. She didn't want to come without permission.

"How about a dance, sweetheart? You look like you need to relax a little."

He stuffed the remote in the pocket of his jeans and held his hand out. Finally, a small reprieve. She took his hand and smiled. She loved dancing, and discreet speakers were blasting out some great country music.

"I'd love to. Let's see if you're a good dancer."

He pulled her into his arms, and they waded onto the full dance floor, her body pressed close to his.

"I'm okay. Caden's the dancer in the family."

He nodded his head toward the other side of the dance floor and Caden twirling an attractive blonde around the floor with some fancy footwork.

"Wow, he's a good dancer. But I think I'll stick with you."

She squeezed his muscled shoulder and gave him her best flirting smile. He pulled her closer in response. She could feel his hard cock pressing against her belly. She rubbed against him, drawing a groan that brought a saucy grin to her lips. She might be the submissive in the relationship, but there was no doubt she wielded her own power, too.

The song changed, and the beat became slower. She recognized the song as Chris Young's "Tomorrow," one of her favorites. Cam had obviously been paying attention. She laid her head on his chest, letting his masculine scent surround her and the beat of his heart mix with the music's rhythm. It was such a sad song. Two people who loved each other so desperately but couldn't make it work. She didn't want it to become the story with her and Cam. She looked up, and his expression was full of passion and tenderness. She swallowed the lump that had suddenly formed in her throat. She couldn't wait a moment longer.

"Cam, I love you. I love you."

His blue eyes darkened, and his throat worked. His arms tightened around her, possessive but gentle.

"I love you, too, baby. I doubt you know how much. I've never felt like this before."

She blinked as tears welled in her eyes. "Me neither. I was afraid you wouldn't say it back, you know."

He shook his head, his lips brushing hers. "No way. I think I fell in love with you the first night at the cabin. You were such an intoxicating mixture of bravado and sweetness. I wanted you from the first minute I saw you in my T-shirt. I'll never stop wanting you."

"I wanted you, too. You were this hot and sexy cowboy. The kind I'd only read about, but you're real."

He took her lips in a long, slow kiss right there in the middle of the dance floor. It was so like Cam to not give a damn about what anyone thought.

"I'm going to show you how real I am tonight. I'm playing for keeps, Noelle."

* * * *

Cam laughed as Noelle blew out the candles on the giant chocolate cake Julie had made for the occasion. It had taken some doing, but she had managed to blow out every candle with pretty much one breath. She had given him a coquettish smile when he told her to make a wish first. He would make it his mission in life to make all her wishes come true from now on. Tonight was only the beginning.

She slowly licked the chocolate icing from the fork, sending his libido into overdrive. He leaned over, ignoring the onlookers, and whispered for her ears alone.

"That pink tongue is going to be put to work tonight, baby. It's been a week since I've been able to use my little submissive."

She turned a becoming shade of pink, and some of the more sharp-eyed observers roared with mirth. She whirled around from the crowd and headed to a table to eat her cake. Cam followed, fingering the remote in his pocket. Maybe his little sub needed to relax. He'd kept her on the edge all night, and it was her birthday after all. He started to press the button when a hand grabbed his sleeve. He turned and felt his irritation start to rise. Gwen.

"Good evening, Cam. Such a lovely night for a party."

Gwen was dressed over-the-top, as usual, in something shiny and completely inappropriate for a barn dance. Her escort, and the reason she was able to come to the party, was Paul Johnson, a friend of Cam's from the club in Bozeman. The man didn't look any damn happier than Cam did. It probably wasn't his first choice for an evening out to go to the birthday party of her ex-husband's new girlfriend. Cam was sure Gwen cared little about Paul's feelings. He was simply her ticket in. Cam was also sure she had come to cause trouble. Something he wasn't going to allow her to do. He and Noelle had exchanged love words. She was under his protection, and he was damned if he'd let his bitch of an ex-wife ruin her party.

"Gwen. Paul. It is a nice evening."

He held out his hand, and Paul shook it with an apologetic look.

"This is a great party, Cam. How've you been? We don't see you at the club anymore."

Cam glanced over at Noelle enjoying her cake. She's seen him with Gwen and had a tiny furrow above her brow. She respected him enough, however, to not run over. He mentally promised to reward her for her circumspect behavior. She was a class act, all the way.

"I'm pretty busy at home these days."

Conversation quickly lagged as they talked about mutual acquaintances. Gwen grabbed onto a pause to inject herself into the conversation. As usual.

"Your new sub is very obedient, Cam. Did you order her to sit and eat her birthday cake like a good little slave?"

Cam looked at the woman who had shared his life and felt nothing. He could only wonder at the man he had been and be glad that man had finally grown up.

"No, but she's a woman who knows how to carry herself in all situations. She doesn't need me to tell her how to act. And she's not my slave, Gwen. And apparently, you're not Paul's either. No Dom would allow your catty behavior."

Paul flushed and pulled Gwen closer. Cam knew his remark had hit home. Paul was a good and decent Dom, but Gwen was running circles around him. He needed to get back in control.

"You're right, Cam. My apologies for my sub. She assured me her behavior would be impeccable. She'll be punished for this behavior."

Cam nodded curtly. "Your best bet is to withhold pain. She acts up to get punished." He turned to head toward Noelle. "It was nice seeing you, Paul. Have a good evening."

He headed toward Noelle, but Colt cut off his path.

"Do you want me to escort them out?"

Cam shook his head, feeling very relieved Gwen wasn't his problem any longer. "No need. I think Paul will have them out of here within minutes. He looked pissed. No Dom likes to be embarrassed by his sub."

Colt snorted. "No man likes to be embarrassed by his woman. Period. Gwen here to cause trouble?"

"Yes, but I'm not going to let her. She's not getting near Noelle. Tonight or any other night."

* * * *

Noelle ducked out for some air. Watching Cam with his ex-wife wasn't her favorite pastime. She wasn't one of those insecure, simpering women who felt the need to latch on to her man when he was talking to another woman, and fuck if she was going to turn in to one. She let Cam take care of his business without her. He could tell her about the conversation later.

"Hiding? Isn't it supposed to be your birthday party?"

Awesome. Gwen was heading right for her. Noelle closed her eyes and held onto the thin thread of her temper. She wasn't the most patient of people at the best of times. She schooled her features and put on her best hostess smile.

"Just getting some air. Can I help you, Gwen?"

Gwen lit a cigarette and blew smoke into the air. She leaned against the building and gave Noelle a thin smile.

"It's really how I can help you. I came out here to give you some advice. I don't know why, but you bring out my protective instincts."

Noelle doubted that with all her heart.

"Really? Well, that's interesting. I'm not sure I'm ready to hear any advice from you, though."

Gwen drew on the cigarette, the tip glowing orange in the dark. "This is friendly advice, I assure you. I think you should know the truth about Cam. And me. It's only right. I don't think it's right for him to deceive you."

"Deceive me? How pray tell has he deceived me?"

Gwen made a show of looking sympathetic, but Noelle wasn't fooled. She'd known women like this and wasn't falling for any of her shit.

"Cam and I, well, we've been talking about getting back together. Right before you came here, we'd decided to give things a try. You see, I wouldn't sleep with Colt, and that was unacceptable to Cam. But now that I've grown older, I see that Cam wants absolute obedience. Submission is everything to him. I can give that to him now. He's just playing with you. After your sister's wedding, he'll let you down gently. He always ends up with me again. How do you think a man like him has stayed single for so long? Has he told you he loves you? He does that with all his temporary subs."

Noelle wanted to grab Gwen by her bleached-blonde hair and drag her to her car and throw her in. This woman had major issues, and God love Cam for having to deal with them over the years. He must have the patience of a saint. She knew better than to feed the fire of Gwen's delusions. She would stand here and try not to make any sudden moves. Thank heaven she didn't have a pet bunny for this woman to boil.

"He wanted you to sleep with Colt, huh? Well, I've already done that for him. Colt is really hot in bed. He's like a stallion. As good as Cam, but in a different way."

Whatever response Gwen had been expecting, this wasn't it. Her mouth gaped open like a fish, and she seemed to have trouble articulating. Noelle smiled.

"I do appreciate the advice, though. Too bad you passed up Colt. He's got a wicked tongue."

Gwen threw her cigarette down and scowled. "Cam is mine. You're just the passing fancy around here. And a slutty one at that."

Noelle shrugged. "I've been called way worse. I think I'll let Cam decide who and what he wants. Are we finished here?"

"Yes," Gwen spat, her face red and not so pretty.

Noelle headed toward the barn as Cam and Colt were hurrying toward her. Cam pulled her into his arms and practically dragged her into a quiet corner, leaving Colt to deal with Gwen.

He placed his hands on her shoulders and gave her a gentle shake.

"What did Gwen say to you? Fuck it all, I swore she wouldn't get near you and dammit, she headed straight for you when our backs were turned. Are you okay?"

Noelle placed her hand on his chest to calm him, but his heart was beating hard and fast under her fingers.

"It's okay." She kept her voice low and soothing. "I admit I was pissed, but I'm fine. She's not that scary, Cam. She's got nothing on the girls in school who teased me for wearing a bra in fourth grade or called me names because of my red hair and freckles. She's strictly amateur hour. She tried telling me that you two were getting back together. She said the reason you split was because she wouldn't have sex with Colt. I didn't believe her, you big, mean Dom."

Cam let his hands drop and took a deep breath. "She said I wanted her to sleep with Colt? Fuck, I never share my subs, and I sure as hell wouldn't share the woman I love. What did you say to her? She looked livid."

Noelle grinned playfully. "I told her I had already slept with Colt for you. I said he was a stallion in bed. As good as you. She called me a slut."

Cam groaned. He looked mad and frustrated, and Noelle wished he would calm down. Gwen kept yanking his chain because she could get a rise out of him.

"That didn't bother you, getting called a slut? And holy hell, Noelle, you told her you slept with Colt. I don't know whether to beat your ass or reward you. Fuck."

Noelle ran her hands around his lean middle and pressed herself close to his warm body.

"My vote is for a reward. And no, a tramp calling someone else a slut doesn't have much sting if you know what I mean."

Cam shook his head and reached into his pocket, pulling out the remote. He pressed the button, sending vibrations through her body and waves of pleasure radiating to her pussy.

"Don't let Julie hear that you said you slept with Colt. She's a jealous woman. Now, come for me, Noelle."

She shuddered and moaned as he held her, the climax cresting and washing over her. It left her shaking and sated against his chest. He lifted her chin with his fingers.

"It's time for your birthday surprise. Let's go, pretty sub."

She let Cam lead her from the party and into his SUV, heading out onto the ranch, far away from their friends and family.

Chapter Ten

The lights from the ranch had already disappeared behind them when he spoke. "We're going to the cabin, sweetheart. Where this all began for us. I can still picture you standing there in the kitchen, wearing my shirt and not much else. I think I fell for you at that moment."

Noelle chuckled and ran her hand along his thighs, feeling his muscles tense under her fingers. "You sure talk sweet for a tough, mean Dom. Going easy on me since it's my birthday?"

"Is that what you want me to do?"

She shook her head. "No, I want my mean Dom to use his sub as he pleases."

Cam caught her hand and lifted it to his lips, brushing her fingertips and sending sparks through her. Her heart tightened with love for him. She couldn't wait to be in his arms, submitting to his desires. She'd come a long way from the woman she was when she arrived. She smiled as she wondered what her creative Dom had in store for her this evening.

They would be alone tonight, and she could make all the damn noise she wanted, no gagging needed. Although if she admitted it to herself, she was starting to enjoy the gag. She was just perverse that way. She giggled as she remembered a show she had seen on television set in the middle of Montana. Perhaps, they wouldn't be completely alone tonight.

Maybe there's a Bigfoot out there.

Cam turned to her with an indulgent smile. "What was the giggle for? You find outdoor life amusing?"

"No, I was just thinking of a show I watched once. It was about hunting for a Bigfoot."

Cam opened the car door with a laugh. "I've lived here pretty much my entire life and never seen one. I guess that doesn't mean they don't exist, though. Maybe we can hunt Bigfoot another night. I have plans for you tonight."

"Hey! You finally got here. Everything's all set for you, Cam."

Noelle was surprised to see Abby and Brody. She was a little disappointed. She loved her sister and Cam's son, but had been looking forward to some alone time with Cam. Abby gave her a big hug.

"Happy birthday, Elle. Brody and I are heading home. If you need anything, call on the radio."

"You're not staying?"

Abby just laughed and shook her head. "Two's company, and four is, well, just kinky. Have fun, you two."

Cam held Abby's door open as she climbed into the car.

"Thanks for helping me with the surprise. We'll see you in the morning."

Noelle entered the cabin and took a good look around. It looked the same, but different tonight. The fire was roaring and keeping everything toasty warm. The table had been set up with a fondue pot on it, surrounded by food for dipping. A giant bouquet of pink roses in a crystal vase stood at one end of the table, giving off an intoxicating scent. To top it all off there were large cushions tossed in front of the fire and a champagne bucket with two glasses.

Her heart started beating faster when she recognized Cam's toy bag in the living area. It had been one long week of recovering from her riding accident, but she was well now and wanted desperately to be with her man.

"What do you think?"

Cam came up behind her and started massaging her shoulders.

She moaned and let her body relax. "I think you have magic

hands. Man, that feels good. I also think you're a freakin' genius. This is just what the doctor ordered."

"I know you might be tired of coming to the cabin, but we can really be alone out here."

Noelle sighed as his hands found a sensitive spot in her neck. "I'm not tired of coming here at all. This place will always be special to me."

He spun her around and gave her a quick, hard kiss.

"Command number one. Go into the bathroom and take off your clothes. You'll know what to do when you get there. We're going to get you to relax right away."

Noelle practically skipped to the bathroom, pushing open the door. She had to catch her breath at the sight before her. The light switch had been taped down. Candles were lit everywhere, casting a romantic glow on the steaming bubble bath just waiting for her. She stripped out of her clothes as quickly as she could and lowered herself into the fragrant water strewn with rose petals. She relaxed back on the bath pillow she was sure Abby was responsible for. This was heaven.

She lost track of time, letting the cares of the world slip away. She was lying there, eyes closed, with a smile on her face when Cam came in.

"Getting relaxed, birthday girl?"

Noelle beckoned to him. "Very. Come join me, handsome."

Cam shook his head. The look on his face made her pussy tingle. He always looked like that before they played. He held up a large bath sheet.

"I have plans for your gorgeous body tonight, and I will not be deviated from my plan. Out of the tub, little sub. Your birthday awaits."

Noelle's nipples tightened, and her cunt gushed cream at the promise in his deep, dark voice. She wanted what only he could give her. She stood up in the tub, the bubbles sliding down her skin, playing peekaboo with her most private parts. One glance at Cam's blue jeans told her he liked what he saw. His big, hard cock was clearly outlined, straining against the tight fabric. She felt a surge of feminine power. It was sweet and heady, and she let it fizz through her veins. She felt beautiful and sexy with this man. She would submit sweetly tonight and take everything he could offer her. To do anything less would only cheat herself.

"Do I please my Dom?"

"You always please me, Noelle. But tonight most especially."

His voice was hoarse with desire, and Noelle stepped out of the tub and into the towel. She stood very still as he dried her gently in some areas and more briskly in others. By the time he was finished, she was aroused and ready.

He traced a line down her cheek all the way to her lips, stroking them with his thumb.

"Do you want to play tonight, little sub? Are you ready to submit to me? Ready for me to push your boundaries?"

She looked deeply into his bluer-than-blue eyes, dark with passion.

"Please, Sir. I want, no, I need to submit to you tonight."

He lifted her into his arms and carried her toward the living room.

"You will, Noelle. Tonight will be one you'll remember for a long time. I'm a man who keeps my promises."

* * * *

Cam carried his woman into the living room and gently deposited her on the cushions. Her birthday night was only beginning. He had so much more in store for her.

"Lie down on your tummy. I'm going to give you a back massage."

She looked like she wanted to say something, but quickly closed her mouth and lay down on the blanket and pillows. He tugged the towel from around her body so she lay naked in the firelight. There was nothing more beautiful than Noelle's gorgeous body highlighted with the soft glow and shadows from the fireplace. Her creamy skin had an opalescent sheen, and he couldn't resist kissing her shoulders where her freckles were sprinkled like pixie dust. He flicked his tongue to taste them and was rewarded with a giggle. He couldn't get enough of her.

He dripped some of Noelle's favorite lotion into his palm and started kneading her muscles. She relaxed underneath his patient hands, hopefully letting the evening slip away. He only wished he was as relaxed. His heart was still beating madly from when he had seen Gwen talking to her. Gwen was trouble with a capital *T,* and he wanted to protect Noelle at all costs. He loved his sons and couldn't regret marrying her. He wouldn't have them otherwise. But he knew Gwen would zero in on Noelle, especially now it was obvious how he felt. He would have to keep them far apart. It shouldn't be too difficult for the next thirty or forty years.

He still couldn't believe how Noelle had handled Gwen. He should have known his mouthy sub wouldn't have any trouble putting Gwen in her place. Still, it was his responsibility. She wouldn't be in this situation except for him. He would let her know he could handle Gwen from now on.

He leaned forward and kissed a wet trail down her delicate spine. She squirmed slightly, a sigh coming from deep in the pile of pillows. He let his tongue wander over her pale ass cheeks. He nipped at one, knowing they would be warm and rosy before long. Then his tongue snaked out to caress her tight little back hole. He pushed her cheeks further apart and pressed his tongue in, drawing a moan from Noelle. She loved the ass play. Tonight he would fuck her there, showing her the pleasure her entire body could bring.

He kissed his way back up her body and nuzzled where her shoulder met her neck, nipping at the sensitive spot. Noelle was wriggling underneath him and giggling in a breathy voice. He ran his hands up her sides from her hips and cupped her full, round breasts, letting his thumb brush the nipples. She immediately lifted her bottom and pressed it to his aching cock. It had been a long celibate week. The evening would be long, too, and nothing turned him on like a sub with her mouth full.

"Turn over, Noelle."

* * * *

Noelle slowly turned over, her entire body languorous after the bath and the massage. Cam was unzipping his jeans and pulling out his enormous cock, already glistening with his pre-cum. He held it in front of her face, and her mouth watered. She wanted it in her mouth. Now.

He stroked it slowly, from root to tip.

"What do you say, little sub?"

Her need to submit was strong tonight. She didn't hesitate to answer.

"May I suck your cock, Sir?"

"Yes, you may. Open wide."

She would have to open wide. His cock was long and thick, and it stretched her jaws to take him. He liked her to take him deep into her throat, and she was getting better each time. He slid over her tongue, and she licked and nibbled at the pulsing veins before taking him farther into her mouth.

His hands tangled in her hair tightly. She loved the feeling of him being in complete control, and she pulled at his hands so he would hold her even more tightly. His other hand came down and splayed at the back of her head.

"Stop playing and suck me, sub."

She started the up-and-down rhythm she knew would send him into orbit. With each stroke, she took him a little deeper. He was bumping the back of her throat, her jaws aching to hold every precious inch of him. She could taste the salty sweetness of his pre-cum as it dripped onto her tongue.

She reached up and fondled his balls, already pulled tight.

"You'll be punished for that, Noelle." His voice was strained and hoarse.

She and only she was bringing him this pleasure. It didn't matter he would punish her for touching him without permission. All that mattered was making him feel amazing. Making him come.

She sped up her efforts, rolling his balls in her hand. She felt him stiffen, and a flood of curse words poured from his mouth. His cock swelled, and then his hot cum was spurting down her throat. She swallowed every drop greedily, hungry for his flavor. She kept licking even after he pulled from her mouth until he groaned and collapsed on the cushions with her. His breath came in harsh rasps, and he sat for long moments recovering.

Finally, his eyes opened, and he gave her the look she was coming to know so well.

"You earned a punishment, Noelle. You've been trained better than that. You know not to touch me without permission. Into the bedroom. I have just the thing for your correction."

Cream flooded her pussy, and she practically ran to the bedroom. She had found a strength she never knew in her submission. She couldn't wait to be punished.

She stopped abruptly inside the door, her jaw dropping. Abby and Brody had woven their magic in here, too. There were more candles, just like in the bathroom, and the bed was strewn with rose petals. But it was the apparatus in the corner of the room that had her full attention. She was pretty certain it hadn't been there on her previous visits.

She walked around it, almost afraid to touch it. Her cunt clenched and leaked honey down her thighs at the thought of what might happen. She looked up as Cam ran his hand across the top.

"It's a bondage table. I had it specially made. It's the perfect height for me. It's also versatile. I can bind you bent over the end or I can have you lying on top."

She reached out and stroked the soft, padded leather on the table.

"This wasn't here last time."

Cam laughed. "Yes, it was. The straps fold flat or under the table. It was sitting in that corner with a cloth draped over it and an arrangement of silk flowers."

Noelle eyed it cautiously. "At the risk of getting punished even worse than I already will, I must ask if you make a habit of bringing subs to this cabin and tying them up."

Cam straightened up, his expression serious. "Fair question. This table used to be in my bedroom. When I divorced Gwen, I said I would never have another sub in my life. So I sent the table here to the cabin. I imagine the boys have used it a time or two."

"Haven't you had lots of subs since your divorce?"

"Yes, but not one special sub, woman, in my life. Not until now."

Noelle smiled. "Then I feel special."

"You are special. A special woman who has a few punishments coming to her."

"A few punishments?" Noelle asked indignantly. "What do you mean a few?"

Cam advanced on her, lifting her chin to look into his blue eyes.

"I told you I had a long memory. Did you think I would forget your transgressions while you were recovering from your accident? I didn't. Tonight you reap what you have sown."

Well, shit.

Noelle lowered her eyes. "Yes, Sir."

Cam barked with laughter. "So submissive. It won't get you out of your punishments. Now bend over the edge of the table like a good girl. I've been looking forward to this for a week."

* * * *

Noelle bent over the edge of the table, her round ass in perfect position for spanking and fucking. Cam knelt down and fastened her ankles to the legs of the table and then fastened her hands out in front of her. She was completely at his mercy now, ass in the air, legs spread. He rubbed the creamy globes of her bottom, already imagining himself balls deep inside her.

Patience.

"Are you comfortable, Noelle?"

She wriggled to get into a better position before answering. "Yes, Sir. I'm comfortable, I guess."

"That didn't sound very convincing. If you're uncomfortable, we should perhaps take your mind off it. What is your safe word, Noelle?"

"Red, Sir."

"Good girl. Now, for your disobedience tonight, ten with the paddle. For your disobedience, including using bad language, during your recovery, fifteen. That's a total of twenty-five. And since it's your thirtieth birthday, let's make it a round thirty plus one to grow on. How would you like the extra, sub? I'm letting you decide since it's your birthday."

There was a small silence. "Belt, please, Sir."

He chuckled. She'd been fascinated with his belt since the day of her riding accident. It was a good choice. He could control the strength of the strokes on what would be a very sore bottom by that time.

"Belt it is, sub. But first, I think we need to warm you up a little."

She was already aroused, but he wanted her good and hot when he started her punishment. She would enjoy it much more when her sense of pleasure and pain were completely skewed.

He knelt and began kissing and licking his way up her shapely legs, the skin warm and smooth under his lips. He nipped at the delicate skin of her inner thigh before taking a lick of the sweet honey dripping from her pussy.

"Oh, Sir!"

He grinned, knowing she loved having her pussy licked, and she loved getting a good, hard spanking. He wanted her to have everything she wanted tonight.

"No coming without permission, Noelle. You know the rules."

He heard her catch her breath right before he dove face-first into her creamy cunt. He licked up all her sweet cream, then went looking for more, as he tongue fucked her tight hole. She was moaning and begging, but she was secured to the table and couldn't get away from his questing tongue. He pressed first one, then two fingers inside her, and she mewled with the pleasure, her muscles tightening on them.

"Do you like having something in your pussy, Noelle?"

"Yes," she hissed.

He pulled his fingers out and pinched her thigh.

"Yes, what, sub?"

"Yes, Sir!"

He pressed his fingers in, and she tried to move her body enough to ride them, but her range of movement was mere millimeters. She was begging in earnest now, her arousal almost at the peak. He was sure she would come from the spanking. He stood up and quickly grabbed the paddle from the dresser. Thank goodness Brody and Abby had set everything up perfectly. He wouldn't be fumbling for toys tonight. He didn't want anything to take away from the scene he was setting for her.

She was trembling with pleasure, and he took a moment to take in how beautiful she looked in the candlelight, restrained for his use and pleasure. He lifted the paddle and brought it down in a controlled fashion on her pale bottom.

She jumped in surprise, and went up on her toes, her breath expelled from her lungs in a whoosh.

"That's one, sub. I'll keep count as I doubt you'll be able to after a dozen or so."

He waited to allow the heat from the stroke to travel straight to her cunt and clit, before raising his arm and bringing it down again. Again she jumped, and he heard her pant. She pulled at the straps on her legs, but they held her firmly. She wanted to press her thighs together against the arousal she was feeling, but she wouldn't have the luxury.

"That's two, sub."

Smack!

Smack!

Smack! Smack! Smack!

Smack!

Smack!

Smack!

"That's ten, sub. That was for touching me without permission. Now on to your other transgressions. Do you need to say your safe word, Noelle?"

"No, Sir." Her voice was breathless, but clear. He could continue, but would keep checking in with her. He ran his fingers through her pussy, and his fingers came away covered in her cream. She whimpered, and he knew she was close to orgasm. *A few more should do it.*

She arched her back, and he knew what she wanted. She needed the paddle to smack her pussy so she could go over. He took careful aim and backed down on the force. It would be the placement, not the strength that made her climax. *One, two...*

"Come for me, Noelle."

Three.

Her body went still, and then he saw the shudders of pleasure rack her slight frame. He stroked her back and whispered soothing words as the orgasm ran through her. When she was coming back to earth, he continued, knowing she could come again before they were finished. He lifted his arm once more and sent a stroke right down on the pillowy cheeks of her rosy ass.

So beautiful.

* * * *

Noelle moaned as her body began its inevitable climb toward orgasm again. He wasn't giving her any respite. After about ten strokes with the paddle, the pain didn't build on itself, only raising the heat on her poor bottom. She was past pink, firmly at red, and knew he wouldn't stop until her ass was white-lightning hot. She'd wanted and needed this, and she was finally getting it.

Each stroke with the paddle sent rods of pleasure straight to her cunt and clit. She needed to come again. Badly.

Finally, he paused, running his fingers over her sore ass cheeks.

"Done with the paddle, sweetheart. I'm proud of you. Do you need to use your safe word?"

She gritted her teeth, her arousal so intense it was painful.

"No, please. I need to come. Please don't stop!"

She was probably topping from the bottom, but at the moment she didn't care. She desperately needed to come, and Cam was what was standing between her and her goal. She couldn't move much in these restraints, but she stood on her toes and arched her back as far as she could, letting him know exactly what she wanted.

He didn't make her wait long. She heard a whistle in the air and then the snap of the belt on her ass. She yelped as the leather made contact with the bright-red skin and part of her pussy. It jacked up her arousal higher. The belt came down again, and she fell over the cliff. She screamed Cam's name over and over as an orgasm stronger than she'd ever known shook every muscle and bone in her body. The waves seemed to last forever, and she vaguely felt the rest of her punishment. The pleasure was too strong for the pain to register, and she rode those waves until they finally left her limp and sated on the table.

His hands petted and soothed her, while he murmured words of praise and love. She didn't protest when a straw was placed between her lips.

"Drink, love. I don't want you to get dehydrated."

She smiled sleepily. "I like it when you call me love, my love."

He grinned. "I like it, too. I like it so much, I'm going to keep calling you that."

She tugged at the straps. "Are you going to let me out of this?"

"Nope. You have to come one more time."

"Is that a rule?"

"There's magic in the number three, sweetheart."

He ran his fingers around her wrists and ankles, checking her circulation. Of course, she was fine since he was an expert at what he was doing. It looked like she was stuck in this position for a while longer. She tried to relax her body, but jumped when she felt the trickle of lube down her crack and his gentle fingers circling her hole. She hissed at the heat in her ass every time his fingers touched the fiery skin. The hiss turned into a moan when his finger breached her tight bottom. He added another finger and began the now-familiar scissoring motion that would stretch her for a plug.

She was surprised when he added a third finger instead of inserting the anal plug. She realized tonight was going to be different. His fingers were brushing those hidden, naughty nerves in her ass, and she bit back her plea for him to fuck her there. She knew well enough he would do as he pleased. She needed to submit to his will and hope it was the same as hers.

She whimpered when he pulled his fingers, leaving her feeling empty and frustrated. She heard the crinkle of a condom wrapper, then the brush of his cock against her sore ass.

"Tonight you'll give me the ultimate submission a woman can give a man. Do you need to use your safe word, Noelle?"

She needed him to fuck her. Hard. Her pussy, her ass, her mouth. It didn't matter, just fuck her. She needed her man's cock deep inside her body like she needed to breathe.

"No, Sir. Please fuck me."

"I will fuck you, love. We won't know where I end and you

begin."

That was exactly what she wanted. His hands gently rubbed her hips and back as the blunt end of his cock pressed at her back hole for entrance. She pushed out as she had been taught, and the head of his cock made it past the tight ring of muscles. The burning and stretching came next, but was bearable. She tried to relax as he relentlessly pushed forward into her dark hole.

She remembered the day she had first seen his cock and thought it would feel like he was splitting her into two pieces if he ever tried to fuck her ass. Well, the day had come, and she indeed felt like her ass, already hot and sore, was being parted like the damn Red Sea. She tried some deep breathing and finally he stopped moving, the pressure easing. She prayed he was all the way in.

He stayed very still, and soon the uncomfortable feeling gave way to pleasure. She liked feeling this full. The pressure was gone, leaving nothing but the tingling she had felt when he had his fingers there. She experimentally moved her bottom, just slightly, and was rewarded with a zing of pleasure from her backside straight to her cunt and clit. She did it again, and this time Cam also groaned his pleasure. She tightened her ass on his cock, and he bit out a filthy word that made her laugh.

"Laughing at your Dom with his cock deep in your ass, are you? Let's see if we can wipe that saucy smile off your face."

* * * *

She was killing him. When she'd tightened her ass even more around his cock, he thought his balls were going to squeeze out his eye sockets. There was nothing like fucking a tight ass, and Noelle's was so snug it was sublime. He was reciting football stats to keep from coming like a teenager. And he was no fucking teenager. He thought he'd learned to control his orgasms long ago. Not with this woman. She was a firecracker, his sweet love. He couldn't wait for them to have a lifetime of this together. It was what he'd hoped for, but never thought he would find at this point in his life.

He pulled out slowly, then thrust in halfway. Pulled out almost all the way, and then thrust in again, a little farther this time. She was moaning and urging him on to fuck her harder and faster. He closed his ears to her entreaties. He wouldn't hurt her, and she was going to be sore tomorrow whether she realized it or not. Each thrust sent pleasure running from his dick, through his balls, to his lower back where it seemed to build and build.

He gritted his teeth and closed his eyes, his cock encased in the hottest, tightest nirvana he could ever have imagined. But this nirvana was real and was going to drive him slowly insane. He built up speed, fucking her hard and fast, just the way she liked it. She was begging him now, and he reached around to her hard, swollen clit and rubbed circles around it. She stiffened, and then screamed her release. Her ass clamped down on his cock, and the pressure in his body became too much to bear. He let go with a growl of pleasure, his body frozen in place. It was like being hit with a freight train and like heaven all at the same time. He shot his seed into the condom, cursing at the thin covering that kept him from marking this woman as his.

He felt primitive with her. She brought out all his he-man instincts when they were together like this. Of course, fucking was one of the most primitive things two people could do.

He slumped over her for a second, then reached and unbuckled her wrists and then her ankles.

"I'll be back in a minute, love. Stay here and I'll take care of you."

He quickly disposed of the condom, washed up, and grabbed a warm cloth for Noelle. She was his to love and care for now. He reveled in the feeling.

She had come up on her elbows and gave him a glassy smile. She was still pretty far gone. He efficiently cleaned her up and carried her over to the bed, cursing the rose petals thrown across it. It had seemed like a romantic idea at the time, but the reality was a little messy. He grinned. A lot like sex. Romantic, but messy.

He held her close, her soft skin pressed against his own. Damn, he loved this woman. He was going to buy Brody and Abby the best wedding present ever as thanks for bringing Noelle to him. She stirred in his arms, giving him a sleepy smile.

"The orgasm was great, Cam. But your bedside manner still needs work. I was left bent over for a long time. You don't want me to get bored, do you?"

He chuckled, rubbing his chin on her shiny red hair. "Are you getting bored? Point taken, love. We have our whole lives for me to find out what bores you and what doesn't."

He held his breath. Was he pushing her too far, too fast? They hadn't discussed commitment past her time here. She'd never mentioned if she wanted to get married. Would she want to have children? He'd love to be a father again.

If she doesn't think I'm too damn old.

She rubbed against him like a cat, yawning in his ear. "Okay. I'm tired. Can we sleep for a while?"

"Of course, baby. You sleep. I'll hold you."

She was already asleep before he finished, her warm breath tickling his neck. She looked like a peaceful angel when she slept, but he knew what a hellion she could be when she was awake. He would have to think of something really inventive and romantic for their next time together. He stayed awake for quite a while watching the flickering shadows and planning their future.

Chapter Eleven

Noelle stretched out on the chaise lounge and watched Cam in the distance working with Brody and Colt. Damn, if her cowboy wasn't hotter than the Fourth of July. She squirmed in her chair, her bottom still slightly sore from the night before. Her birthday sex had been fucking amazing. When she'd woken later, he'd held her tenderly on his lap while feeding her from the fondue on the table. She had nibbled at angel food cake dipped in chocolate and then on his tasty lips.

This morning, before they'd headed back to the house, he had sheepishly handed her a package. They'd been so absorbed in each other, he'd forgotten to give her the birthday present he'd picked out for her.

She'd ripped into it like a five-year-old on a cupcake. She loved presents, and this one didn't disappoint. It was a gift certificate for both her and Abby to visit a spa for a day of pampering before the wedding. She and Abby were already making plans. They were both girly girls, and this was one present that would be put to good use.

"I swear Brody is just sexy as all hell when he's out working on the ranch. He gets all sweaty and looks so manly. I'm going to molest him tonight," Abby said in her best cowboy drawl. "Damn, he is fine."

Noelle eyed her man in his tight blue jeans and sweaty shirt. He could make her tingle with just one look.

"I don't know about Brody, but my man is sexier than sin. And you better not let Brody hear you cursing. He's as bad as Cam about punishing unladylike language."

Abby laughed. "I've got Brody wrapped around my finger. I just bat my eyelashes and tell him how sorry I am and how I need to be punished and he just melts into a puddle. Brody's just a baby Dom compared to Cam. I don't think I would try that on Cam, if I were you."

"I've tried it, and it doesn't work, but more power to you."

The men were heading toward the house, and Noelle's body started to hum as Cam approached. It remembered last night vividly. He knelt down next to her and brushed her lips with his.

"Hey, sweetheart. What are you working on?"

Before Noelle could answer, Brody pulled Abby out of her chair with a whisper in her ear. It looked like Abby wasn't going to need to molest Brody after dinner. He was going to do it for her, right now.

She lifted up her sketchbook for his perusal. "I'm working on designing a new jewelry line. I actually got the idea from Abby's collar. It's a line of BDSM jewelry. This is a collar I've been working on."

"Honey, that's really beautiful."

He ran his fingers along the base of her neck slowly.

"It would look good on you. A gorgeous sub should be adorned with a gorgeous collar."

Noelle pulled a face. She hated things around her neck. They chafed and bothered her. If she wore a necklace, it had to have a long chain.

"I'm not really the collar type."

The expression on his face changed immediately, closing down and looking remote. He was taking her statement completely wrong.

"It's not what you're thinking. I just don't like choker-type necklaces. This is more of what I would want."

She flipped over a few pages to the drawing she had been working on all morning. It was a belly chain encrusted with amethysts, which were her birthstone, and blue topaz, which was Cam's birthstone. There was also a diamond-studded tag and carefully placed rings for attaching leashes or other chains. She was already picturing herself wearing it.

He looked at the drawing for a long time. "That would look amazing on you. Very sexy. And all mine."

She cupped his cheek. "I'm not saying I'm ready for something like this. We haven't known each other long. I'm just saying that if we get to this point, well, I hate stuff around my neck. Just sayin'."

He quirked an eyebrow. "Just sayin', huh? Can I have that drawing? For some time in the future. Maybe. Just sayin'."

She smiled and pulled the page from the sketchbook. She had designed it for them in mind, in truth. He folded it up and tucked it in his pocket.

"How about a date night, sweetheart? We could go into town and have dinner. Maybe see a movie. We can work on getting to know each other even better."

"Do I get to wear panties?"

"Nope."

She leaned forward and kissed him softly. "Then I'm definitely in."

* * * *

Noelle laughed, taking a big bite of her chicken marsala. She and Cam had seen a movie earlier and were now enjoying dinner at a small Italian restaurant.

"The movie was terrible, Cam. There is no way the hero fell off the scaffolding and grabbed onto the tree limb to catch himself. He would have ripped his arm out of the socket. And that's just one example. I could go on all night."

Cam shook his head and smiled. "I have no doubt you could, love. Let's just agree that I suspend disbelief easier than you do. Next movie we see will be a grim documentary. Will that be believable enough for you?"

She stuck out her tongue playfully. She was having so much fun with Cam tonight. She had even convinced him to make out in the back row of the movie theater for a few minutes. She was pretty sure the two old women sitting in front and off to the side had enjoyed the show. They had given Cam a bright, flirty smile on the way out of the theater, much to his chagrin. He had promised her a spanking when they got home which they both knew was no threat. Noelle loved her spankings.

Cam reached for her hand with a serious expression.

"Sweetheart, I think we need to have a talk. A talk about our relationship."

Noelle's heart started beating a little faster. "Is this the 'It's not me, it's you' speech?"

"Fuck, no. I love you. I meant that. I want to talk about what we intend to do about this. The wedding is coming up, and I know you have a life in Florida. A life I'm guessing you want to get back to."

Noelle bit her lip, wanting to say just the right words. "I do miss my life. I love my friends, my business, and my little condo on the beach."

She squeezed his hand. "But. I've fallen in love with not only you, but your family and the ranch. Listen, I've been thinking about this. You obviously can't move to Florida. Your work is here. But my work is portable. That's the main reason I was able to pick up and come here to help Abby. Not that she really needed my help. She had everything under control."

"She didn't have you. She wanted her sister, I'm guessing at this special time of her life."

"You're probably right. I'm glad she asked me. If she hadn't, I'm not sure you and I would have had enough time to fall in love if I just came for the wedding and left."

Cam shook his head. "I was attracted to you at first sight. I would have found a way to get to know you. I would have found a reason for you to come back and visit. This was meant to happen, sweetheart."

She loved when he talked like this. She loved him. "I was thinking

I could start planning to move my business here, and put my condo up for sale. But I'd like to wait a few months so we can get to know each other better. So far, everything is great, but I'd like to experience more of this dominance and submission. I think I could do this for a lifetime, but I need to be sure. That will take time. I'm happy to travel back and forth for a while. Would you agree to that?"

Cam's shoulders relaxed. "This was better than I hoped for, honestly. I was afraid we might be at a stalemate, living thousands of miles away from each other. Committing to a D/s relationship is a big step, and I'm glad that you're taking it seriously. I'm also grateful that you're willing to be open to relocating. And I won't make you do all the traveling. I've wanted a vacation in Florida. I'll take you to Disney."

Noelle rolled her eyes. "I have annual passes. I'll take you to Disney, cowboy."

Cam swirled his wineglass and looked nervous. It wasn't a usual look for her arrogant, bossy Dom. Finally he spoke, "Disney's a good place for children. How do you feel about children?"

"Children in general, or having children, in particular?"

Cam still looked guarded. "Having children, in particular. With me, specifically."

For a moment, Noelle thought about teasing him, but then took pity on him. He looked almost terrified of her answer.

"I've always wanted to have a few kids. I thought it would be fun to have a couple of boys, actually."

He seemed to relax slightly. "You're in luck. Boys seem to be all I can make."

"All three of your sons seem to be fine men. It's obvious you were a good dad." She set her wineglass down. They needed to get to the heart of the matter.

"Are you asking because you'd like to have more children or because you're done having children?"

He looked deep into her eyes, and she could see his vulnerability.

"I thought I was done having children, until I met you. If our relationship continues to progress over these next few months, I wondered if you would consider having a baby, or two, with me. I'm still young, or at least I still feel young. I'm in good health, and I don't mind changing diapers or 2:00 a.m. feedings."

"That's good because I don't do well when I miss sleep." She reached over and grabbed his hand. "I'm going to answer your real question. No, I don't think you're too old to be a father again. I think you would make a great dad. To my kids specifically. No one else's. Okay?"

He seemed relieved. "Okay. It's not easy asking your woman if she thinks you're too old."

Noelle rolled her eyes and giggled. "If I said you were too old, you'd just spend the entire night proving to me how young you still are. I'd like to be able to walk tomorrow, if you don't mind."

Noelle saw a familiar face out of the corner of her eye. She smiled and pointed toward the door. "Look, John just came in. I didn't know he'd be in town tonight."

Cam twisted around and gave a wave. "I didn't either."

John's expression turned to one of shock then horror. He turned and headed back out the entrance he had just come through. Cam chuckled.

"Being a teenager is a nightmare. He probably didn't want his friends to see his family. I remember not wanting any of my friends to even know I *had* family, let alone be in the same movie theater or restaurant together."

"My teen years don't hold fond memories for me either. But weren't you the big man on campus?"

"Just because I was popular in high school didn't make it any easier."

"Yeah, it must have been awful having all those blonde cheerleaders throwing themselves at you."

"The only woman I want throwing herself at me is right here.

Speaking of that, are you wearing panties?"

Noelle gave him an evil smile and raised her eyebrows. "I think we should finish dinner and you should take me home and find out."

Cam tucked into his meal with gusto. "Sounds like a plan. I've got a paddle and gag with your name on it."

* * * *

Cam's cock was harder than a fence post by the time they arrived back at the ranch house. Noelle had been one naughty submissive on the way home, teasing him by touching herself as he had driven down the long, dark road that led home. Even though she hadn't removed a stitch of clothing and was only touching herself through the fabric, it had turned him on so hard he could barely keep the car on the road. He had vowed her bottom would be bright red, and she'd be on her knees servicing his cock, but she had just laughed and ran her fingers around her hard nipples, poking through her blouse, and drawing his eyes from the road.

He'd known she was trying to get his mind off running into Gwen as they had exited the restaurant. Surprisingly, Gwen had been less than enthused to see him, too. She had ducked into the building as if she hadn't seen him, when clearly she did. He was relieved she wasn't going to make a scene with Noelle there. He had meant it when he told her it was his job to protect her from his ex.

He grabbed her hand as they climbed the porch steps. A picture of them growing old together and sitting, holding hands on that very same porch seemed so vivid it took his breath away. She was a woman he wanted in his life. He couldn't wait to show her over the next months how much he loved her and wanted her here, by his side, sharing his life.

Shouts coming from the house made him pause outside the door. The house was always boisterous, but the voices inside were angry. Noelle gave him a questioning look, and he shrugged and pushed open the front door. It was clear from the tension and body language, Abby and Brody were having a pre-wedding lover's quarrel.

"I'm going to turn you over my knee and beat your bottom until you behave!"

"The hell you will! You can't take what I'm not willing to give. I'm not getting a spanking because you're being an insensitive asshole!"

His son's face was beet red.

"You'll get a spanking, all right. You won't be able to sit for a week. I won't have my sub questioning my judgment."

"Someone has to, you stupid jerk. I'll be damned if your ex-girlfriend is coming to our wedding."

"I invited her, and that's that."

"Then uninvite her or there won't be a wedding. And that's that."

As much as Cam wanted to intervene and tell his son he actually *was* being an insensitive asshole, Brody needed to learn how to handle his woman on his own. There were times for being the Master of the home, and times to fucking duck and run when the woman in your life was on the warpath.

Apparently, Noelle had no such reticence. She walked right in between the couple and put her hands up in a stop motion. Miraculously, both Abby and Brody immediately shut up and paid attention.

"Stop it, both of you. You're supposed to get married in a week, and here you are arguing like you hate each other."

Brody pointed to Abby. "She said—"

Noelle cut him off with a wave of her hand. "Hush. Now. I don't care what you did, and I don't care what she said. You will lower your voices and speak respectfully to one another. Now, Abby, why are you angry with Brody? And speak nicely, please."

Abby's pretty face screwed up, and tears started rolling down her pale cheeks.

"Br–Br–Brody ran into his ex-girlfriend who's visiting in town, and he invited her to the wedding."

Abby scrubbed at her face. His son was quickly melting as he watched the woman he loved become increasingly miserable.

"When I met him, he had just broken up with her, and all his friends said she was the love of his life. I don't want the love of his life at our wedding. He's cruel to invite her."

Abby choked as she tried not to sob. Brody didn't look in much better shape. His whole body was sagging, and his face was paper white.

"Aw, fuck, baby. She's not the love of my life. You are. You're the only woman I've ever really loved. That's why I didn't think it was a big deal if she came to the wedding. I don't feel anything for her. How can I? You're my world, sweetheart. Please don't say I'm cruel. Please don't stop loving me because I'm stupid."

Abby pushed past Noelle and threw herself at Brody. "I haven't stopped loving you, you big, dumb Dom. But you have pissed me off royally. You don't get to make all the damn decisions for the rest of our life because you're the Dominant."

Noelle was smiling and looking pretty pleased with herself. Cam walked up behind her and put his hands on her shoulders. As much as he was proud of her for getting Abby and Brody to stop fighting, the young couple would need to learn to deal with each other eventually without his or Noelle's intervention. Marriage was something a couple had to constantly work at.

Cam cleared his throat. "This is just my opinion, and I know many in the lifestyle who would tell me I'm completely wrong. But a marriage, even a Dominant-submissive marriage, is a partnership first and foremost. Decisions and boundaries should be discussed and negotiated. The Dominant should only press his will beyond those boundaries when he feels the decision is for his sub's safety or well-being."

Brody's head was hanging and he was studying his fingernails.

"I guess I forgot that. I may have gotten carried away with being the one with the power."

Noelle cocked her head to the side and looked puzzled. "I know I haven't been here very long, but from what I've seen and experienced, the sub has all the real power."

His smart little sub had figured it out, and within weeks, too. A Dom could only take what a sub gave willingly, and she had the power to stop everything with one word. It was a good lesson for the young Dom.

He squeezed her shoulders. "True, Noelle. Doms have what I like to call 'given' power. The power is given to them by the sub. The sub can take it back at any time. This is not the same as disobedience, and you shouldn't confuse the two. If Abby doesn't want to give Brody the power to make all the decisions, they need to negotiate what decisions he is empowered to make."

Everyone stood frozen. Cam sighed and shook his head. "Now would be a good time to do that."

The young couple finally cracked a small smile and headed outside for what Cam hoped would be a very long walk and talk. He wanted to get his sexy woman upstairs and naked. He pulled her back against him, her warm, womanly scent teasing his nostrils.

"I want you upstairs, and I want you naked. Get on all fours on the bed and wait for me."

He was totally serious, and when she realized it, she smiled and fled up the stairs. He chuckled as he watched her round little fanny retreat, and his cock hardened in response. He was going to make love to his woman until she couldn't walk.

Chapter Twelve

Noelle waited on all fours in their bedroom. She had run upstairs and stripped as quickly as she could, but she needn't have bothered. Cam was going to keep her waiting tonight. She was in his favorite submissive position. He never made her get on her knees. He preferred her posed like this, ready to suck or be fucked. Her pussy was already creaming and clenching as she waited, ass in the air, facing the wall away from the door. Cam was exacting in his requirements.

She heard the door swing open but didn't turn her head, keeping her eyes trained on the headboard. She heard him set something down on the nightstand and then the rustle of fabric as he removed his clothes. She stayed frozen until he came into her line of sight. His cock was already hard, and she wanted to reach out and stroke the velvety skin. Her mouth watered as she imagined his flavor dripping on her tongue while he fucked her mouth.

"Kneeling position, sub."

She quickly came off her arms and stayed on her knees. He set several toys in front of her, and arousal went zinging through her veins. It was going to be a hot night with her cowboy.

"The gag is non-negotiable. You're a screamer, and we can't wake up the entire ranch. Pick a toy or two, sweetheart."

She trembled with excitement as she pointed to the nipple clamps and then his belt, tossed carelessly on the bedroom floor. He nodded and scooped up the plugs and dildos, leaving out the gag, a wooden box, and the now-familiar leather cuffs, then picking up the belt and tossing it on the bed. He reached for the cock gag and held it in front of her face. It had deep gouges in the plastic where she had bit into it last time as he had held her on the edge of orgasm for what had seemed like hours.

"Open, sub."

She opened, and the cock slid in, stretching her jaws wide. He fastened it firmly behind her and patted her bottom in praise.

"Good girl. You look so beautiful with your mouth full, you can't imagine."

She loved it when he gagged her. At first, she had found the gag uncomfortable, but her perverse nature had kicked in, and now she loved the feel of her mouth stretched and full. She only wished it was his real cock, not a fake, plastic imitation.

He pressed the squeaky toy into her hand.

"You shouldn't need this tonight, but we won't take any chances. Wrists, please."

She held out her wrists, and he swiftly and efficiently wrapped the soft, leather cuffs around them. He reached for the clamps.

"I'm glad you chose these tonight. Your nipples look so pretty when they're clamped. I know how sensitive you are there. Maybe we can get you to come just from breast stimulation."

She loved the rituals of the cuffs and gag. Her pussy was already swollen and burning, needing to be fucked hard by his big cock. Only Cam knew when that time would come tonight. She could only wait and hope her good behavior made the length of time shorter.

He bent and sucked an already-hard nipple into his warm, wet mouth. She groaned against the cock pressing her tongue down as he scraped his teeth and nipped until it stood tight and erect. He repeated the process on the other side and let his fingertip draw circles around the pink areolas. She pressed her thighs together to stave off her building orgasm. He could easily get her to climax with just his mouth and tongue.

He dangled the clamps in front of her, a chain connecting them.

"I think you'll find these interesting."

He opened the clawlike teeth and quickly snapped them shut on each nipple. She closed her eyes as the burn shot through her body. She tried to even her breathing until she felt the pleasure build, finally opening her eyes. His eyes were focused on her with laser intensity. She knew she was completely safe with this man. He was always watching her reactions. If he thought for one second she didn't like what was happening, she knew it would come to a complete halt.

He played with the silver chain dangling between her breasts, then pulled it up and hooked it the gag. She was so surprised, she moved her head abruptly and jerked the chain, pulling at her tender nipples. Cream flooded her needy pussy. Her diabolical Dom had found a way to allow her to control the pain of the clamps. If she needed a push in arousal, she only needed to move her head.

"You like that, don't you, sub? Pull at them again for me."

Her nipples were already burning, but she lifted her chin and gave them a tug with her head. The pain shot through her and straight to her cunt and clit, quickly transforming on the way to the utmost pleasure. She did it again before he could stop her.

"Easy there, sweetheart. Not too hard, or you'll tear. Your slightest movement will pull at them. Now let's get you into position."

He pulled each wrist straight back and fastened them behind her back. She was now helpless, ass in the air, kneeling on the bed.

"You love being in bondage, don't you, sub?"

She nodded, the chain pulling at her nipples sending arrows of pleasure through her veins. He pushed at her thighs so they were spread wide apart. The cool air blew against her heated cunt, but didn't pull her back from the edge. She needed to come soon.

He lay down on the bed and scooted under her, pushing her thighs even wider so her pussy was right on top of his mouth. His breath was hot and moist against her clit and his tongue snaked out and gave it a long, slow lick. She would have screamed with the pleasure if she hadn't been gagged.

His tongue moved lazily up and down her slit, through the folds, everywhere but where she needed it most. His hands were like steel bands around her quivering thighs and kept her from grinding her pussy on his face. She almost went over when he pressed two fingers in her drenched cunt.

"You do not have permission to come, sub."

Thankfully, he didn't understand her profanity-laced reply. She was one big mass of need on the edge and he wouldn't give her permission.

"I don't know exactly what you just said, sub, but I'm guessing you just questioned my parentage. You'll be punished for that."

He ran his tongue in circles around her clit and then tongue fucked her gushing hole. She bit into the cock in her mouth to hold off her orgasm. She whimpered when he pulled his mouth away, and felt the tug on her clamped nipples. The pleasure rippled through her like water. She was a hair's breadth away from release. She tried to gulp air, but the gag kept her from taking a big breath. She felt his work-roughened hand stroke her spine.

"Relax, sub. Concentrate on your breathing. Get control of your body."

She finally had her breathing even and calm when he lifted up the belt lying near her head on the bed. Her heart sped up, and her pussy dripped more honey down her thighs. She loved the feel of his leather belt on her bare bottom.

"You'll get ten tonight. Five because of what you called me when your gag was in and five because I love how your ass looks when it's bright red."

She waited for the first strike. He loved making her wait, drawing out the tension as long as he could. This was part and parcel of her submission. She would lie here with her ass in the air as long as he decided she needed to. When she thought she couldn't take anymore, she finally heard the whistle of the belt in the air and felt the leather make contact with her flesh. A stripe of heat ran across her ass cheeks. She had jumped with the first stroke and tugged at her sore nipples, making her shiver and whimper. He let the heat from her bottom travel to her cunt before the second stroke, placed neatly above the first. Once again she jumped and once again she pulled on the chain linked to the clamps. She whimpered and moaned with the need to come.

"Eight more, sub. Try to stay still or you're going to make your nipples hurt worse than they need to."

Three more strokes were laid in horizontal stripes across her ass, adding to the burning heat in her bottom and pussy. He reached out and ran his fingers through her creaming cunt. She groaned at the contact.

"Come for me, sub."

It took two more strokes low on her ass at the crease of her thighs to send her over. The gag muffled her scream as her body was shaken by wave after wave of pleasure. She was about to come down when he reached under her and unclamped her nipples before continuing her punishment, giving her the last three strokes and sending her into another climax that left her spent and dizzy. The blood rushed into the burning tips of her breasts and seemed to intensify the pleasure a thousandfold. Soon she was slumped on the bed, ass and nipples on fire.

He whispered words of praise in her ear and stroked her hair back from her face.

"You're amazing, Noelle. I'm so proud of you. Let's see how your body responds to something completely different."

He flipped open the box and revealed its contents. Long fluffy feathers. He pulled one from the box and let it trail down her spine, down her crack, to her back hole. She jerked against the light tickles and pulled vainly at her cuffs. She was held fast.

His eyes crinkled with his smile. "You're afraid of a few feathers? Would you rather be whipped than tickled?"

Noelle nodded vigorously. She feared the feathers most of all. He just smiled wider, her evil Dom.

"Give it a chance, sweet sub. If you don't like it, squeeze your toy."

She loved it and hated it at the same time. He ran that damn feather all over her sensitized flesh. Tickling her and starting her climb to orgasm all over again. He traced patterns on her sore ass and circled her tight rosette. Then, he reached under her and tickled her throbbing nipples, sending sticky honey trickling down her thighs. He stopped to wipe up a drip with his fingers and sucked them clean.

"Sweet. I love eating your pussy. I love fucking it even more. But first things first."

He reached back in the box and pulled out two feathers, less fluffy than the last. They were narrower, with stiffer bristles. Her pussy and ass clenched at what he might do with them. He began running them up and down her cunt, amping up her arousal and sending her all the way to the edge.

"I think you're going to really love this."

She screamed silently as he pressed the two feathers inside her dripping pussy, swirling them against all the sensitive nooks and crannies, especially her G-spot. He kept up the rhythm until she thought she would die from the pleasure. Finally, she heard his firm, deep voice.

"Come, sub."

She threw back her head and let go, her orgasm hitting her sideways. Her teeth sunk into the gag as pleasure so intense it was painful racked her body. He pulled one of the feathers from her cunt and tickled her swollen clit until she was rocking back and forth on her knees with pulses of light and dark behind her eyes. Her world was turned upside down and then righted again as she came down slowly. She didn't want the pleasure to end, but somehow she couldn't even keep her eyes open. She didn't even realize when her cuffs were unclipped and the gag removed. She was pulled close to his warm, muscular body.

She drifted for an unknown period of time before opening her eyes. His blue gaze collided with hers. He was always watching her, making sure she was okay. She reached up and ran her fingers over his full lips, punishments be damned. They were calling to her, and she liked the punishments anyway. He opened his mouth and nipped her with his teeth, before leaning down and kissing her long and hard, leaving her wanting and breathless. How could she be this ready to be fucked when she had already come twice?

He ran his hand down her back and cupped her sore ass cheek.

"There's magic in the number three, pretty sub. On your back, hands over your head."

* * * *

Cam let his gaze rove over the beautiful woman he loved. Her skin had a rosy glow from her orgasms, her hair tossed and wild around her shoulders like a flame. He couldn't stop himself from cupping her round, creamy breasts and taking a taste from her pink nipples. She moaned as he licked and nipped at what he knew would be sensitive, sore flesh. He would command her not to wear a bra tomorrow.

He lifted her arms and clipped them to the headboard. He didn't care if her nails shredded his back, but she loved the restraints and admitted she came harder when she was in bondage. He leaned back, letting his hands run from her shoulders down to her ankles.

"You are not to come until I give you permission, sub."

He scooted up her body so his cock was right in front of her full, lush lips.

"Suck me."

She licked her lips, and his cock tightened and hardened further. Holding back had been painful, but he wanted to push Noelle's boundaries while she was here. He hid his chuckle. He could always grab a quickie in the shower later or in the morning. She was always wet and ready for him, not because he had told her to be. She was ready for him because she loved this as much as he did. She drank in the pleasure and gave him the same. This wasn't sex. This was making love at its finest. He'd never had it this good.

Her mouth opened, and her pink tongue lapped at the mushroom head of his cock, where his pre-cum dripped from the slit. He pulled back just enough so her tongue couldn't reach him.

"I said suck, sub."

She nodded, and he moved closer until the warmth of her mouth enfolded his cock. He bit back a groan as he slid over her tongue, bumping the back of her throat. His hand went to the back of her head, lifting her so she could take him deeper. He thrust in and out, her tongue flitting with each stroke until his balls were pulled tight and he knew he would blow his load into her mouth if he didn't stop. He pulled out despite her protests.

"Not there, love. I want to come in your sweet pussy."

He snagged a condom and pulled her legs over his shoulders. She would feel more at his mercy in this position, and she loved that. He nudged her cunt with the head of his cock before pulling back and plunging in with one hard stroke. She gave out a half scream at his impalement. He was balls deep, and he gritted his teeth to fight the urge to come like a teenager on his first date. He thought about ice, snow, and tax policy. He finally had himself under control and began to move, slowly at first, knowing it drove her mad.

She liked it hard and fast, and he moderated his strokes, making sure each one rubbed her swollen clit and hit her G-spot. She was mewling under him, urging him on, and he couldn't deny this woman the pleasure she had no shame in asking for. He sped up, thrusting hard, slamming her cunt each time. She was pulling at her cuffs, calling him her big cowboy Dom and telling him to pound her hard and faster.

The filthy talk spurred him on and to the edge. He leaned down and whispered in her shell-like ear.

"Come, my love."

He swallowed her screams of ecstasy with his mouth. Her pussy clamped down on his cock, and that was all it took to send him over, too. Each shudder of pleasure from her body shook him to the core. He emptied his seed in the condom before slumping on top of her, spent and delirious with happiness. His woman was amazing, and he was one lucky cowboy Dom.

He pulled away regretfully, unclipping her cuffs and disposing of the condom quickly. He brought back a warm cloth and cleaned her sticky thighs, and she didn't protest once. He smiled as she fought to keep her eyes open.

"Sleep now, love. I'll wake you in a few hours for round two. I'm going to fuck you so hard you won't be able to walk tomorrow."

Her eyelashes fluttered but she smiled back. "Promises, promises."

"This is a promise I guarantee you I'll keep."

He woke her up a few hours later, not bothering with any restraints or toys. It was just the two of them, their bodies pressed close. He wanted to let her know without a doubt, he was still young enough to love her all night long. She let him know she was old enough to let herself go and not feel a moment of guilt for all the naughty, raunchy things they did in the middle of the night.

Chapter Thirteen

His impressive cock pushed forward relentlessly against the barrier of her virginity. He pulled back for a moment, his gaze never leaving her face, before thrusting in to the hilt. She cried out as she became a woman. His woman. He stayed very still while she grew used to being filled by him. A lone tear ran down her cheek. He brushed it away softly.

He began to move, slowly at first, then building up speed. She gripped his shoulders and wrapped her legs around his lean waist. Her body was humming with the pleasure, and she felt it building, but toward what she had no idea.

He leaned forward and captured her lips with his own, his tongue seeking and playing with hers. Each thrust of his body was sending her higher, and she raked her nails across his back as something inside her shattered. The pieces flew, and she flew along with them. She was soaring, and when she finally came down she knew what everyone was talking about. This was love. She had made love.

Brianne scrunched up her face and reached for her martini glass. "Um, I don't know about you all, but my first time wasn't like this at all. It hurt like a bitch, and I sure as hell didn't have an orgasm. I wasn't even close."

Lisa pushed the chocolate box toward Tori. "I didn't have an orgasm until I was with Conor. This poor girl thinks sex and orgasms are love. He'll probably dump her like last week's trash. Asshole."

Tori popped a dark chocolate into her mouth. "My first time was okay. It hurt but not too bad. But it was embarrassing, you know? No one, except maybe Judy Blume, tells you how damp and messy sex can be."

Noelle cracked up. "Thank heaven for Judy Blume. If it hadn't been for her, I don't think I would have known much about sex. My parents sure as hell never had the talk with me. Did yours?"

Lisa rolled her eyes. "My mother only talked to me about sex once. When one of our neighbors went crazy and started running around the neighborhood naked, yelling the Russians were coming, she took the opportunity to point out his penis and tell me I should stay away from all penises. Penises were bad apparently."

Brianne laughed. "My mother said just about the same thing only more hysterically, like they carried the cold and flu virus. Did your neighbor just see *Red Dawn* or something?"

Lisa sipped her martini. "I think it was *The Day After*, but I'm not sure. It was the eighties, and everyone was paranoid."

Tori pushed the box of chocolates away. "No more chocolate for me. I need to start training for Gasparilla."

Noelle had her own box of chocolates from Cam. "I don't know how you can run like that. If anyone ever sees me running, you'll know it's the Zombie Apocalypse."

"Montana should be a pretty safe place from the Zombie Apocalypse." Lisa laughed. "Might you be living there full-time in the near future?"

Noelle shook her head. "Not the near future. Cam and I talked, and I'm going to travel back and forth for a few months. I think we need to take some time and really get to know one another. In the meantime, I can start to investigate moving my business and maybe selling my condo. If everything works out, of course."

Brianne nodded in approval. "It's nice to see this side of you, Elle. Usually you're full steam ahead. Taking some time certainly can't hurt."

"I know I can be impetuous, but this is serious. I want to do this right. Heck, maybe I'm finally growing up now that I'm with Cam."

Lisa yawned dramatically. "How perfectly boring. We like you the way you are, Elle."

"Awww, that's sweet, Lisa. But according to Tori and Brianne, maturity is its own reward."

"I never said that," Brianne protested.

Tori's cheeks were pink. "I may have, and I was full of shit. Don't grow up because you think you need to for Cam. If he doesn't love you the way you are, then he isn't worth it."

"He does love me the way I am, and he is worth it. It's just strange that now I'm happily in love, I feel, well, more settled. I don't feel rushed. It seemed like before I was always in a hurry."

Tori stretched out her long legs and gave Noelle a mischievous smile. "If I had that hunky cowboy, I'd be in a hurry. In a hurry to get him naked. Where is he today anyway? Last time we got to get a glimpse of him."

Cam had met all the women during last week's book club meeting. They had all fawned over him, of course.

"Working, as usual. Now that the weather's warmer, he said they work from sunup to sundown. In fact, I think I need to wrap up here and go help with dinner."

Brianne closed her e-reader. "Me, too. Kade is going through a growth spurt and eating me out of house and home."

Lisa sighed. "I guess that means I have to feed my children, too. What about you, Tori?"

"Two teenage boys means I'm always cooking. But it was good to get together today. Elle, when are you coming home? We should do a girls' night."

"The wedding is next week, then I'll be on a plane. But I'll be coming back here very soon."

Tori smiled. "True love. I miss it."

Lisa's expression was serious. "We need to find you a man, Tori. You shouldn't be alone."

Tori shook her head. "I'm concentrating on the boys. I'm not ready."

Brianne put her hand on Tori's shoulder. "You just let us know when you are. Nate has some very nice, single doctor friends we can fix you up with."

"Or some Montana cowboys." Noelle laughed. "I can vouch for how hot the men are out here."

"I'm not ready. You'll all be the first to know when I am."

Lisa smiled. "Get ready, Tori. You're next."

* * * *

Noelle nudged her horse on, shivering when a cold, nasty wind almost knocked her sideways. This horseback ride wasn't turning out like she had planned. She hoped she could reach her destination before the heavens opened up and the rain came down.

She'd been surprised after the book club meeting to find a note on the bed from Cam telling her to saddle a horse and head toward where she had been thrown mere weeks before. Surprised, but pleased. Her body had flushed with heat as she wondered what surprises he might have in store for her. She had already fantasized a cozy tent and a few sex toys. She could scream in ecstasy as much as she wanted out here, and no one would hear her.

However, the weather was not cooperating. Dark clouds had gathered, and the wind had picked up quite a bit. Her long hair was getting whipped around, and she wished she had brought more than this thin jean jacket. Cam was going to have to keep her warm as soon as she saw him, which was why she was urging her horse to keep going. Even Poncho was wondering about the wisdom of this little adventure. He wasn't as skittish as Turismo, but he was just as ornery. He definitely had a mind of his own. And his mind was not happy about the slicing wind that was coming out of the west.

She pulled on the reins and looked around. She had assured Abby she could find the spot without trouble, but now she was wondering if perhaps she had taken a wrong turn. The cluster of trees she had thought she remembered well was nowhere in sight. Or perhaps it was that all the trees looked the same. Add in the darkening sky and her nervousness about the weather and she was starting to feel like she was well and truly screwed.

And not in a good way.

A clap of thunder overhead made her jump, but luckily Poncho seemed unconcerned. At least he wouldn't be throwing her off and bolting for sweet oats in the barn when the going got rough. Another glance at the ever-darkening sky made her chew her lip with nervousness. Cam had left her a note to meet him. She wanted time alone with him in the worst way. But, the worsening weather was telling her to turn around and head back to the ranch. Cam was just going to have to understand. Her mind made up, she turned Poncho around and headed back in what she hoped was the direction of the ranch. She prayed she'd get there before the storm turned really bad.

* * * *

Cam breathed a sigh of relief as he pulled the back door of the ranch house open. Sheets of rain were falling practically sideways, and he was soaked after coming in from one of the pastures. He couldn't wait to get warm with a hot bath, a cold beer, and a hot woman. He shook the rain from his hat and looked around the kitchen. Abby was humming and making dinner, but Noelle was nowhere in sight.

He pulled off his soaked boots and threw them next to the door.

"Abby, dinner smells great. I'm headed to take a hot shower. Is Noelle upstairs or still in my office on Skype with her girlfriends?"

Abby swung around with a frown, holding a spatula.

"What are you doing here?"

Poor Abby must have had a case of terrible bridal nerves. Thank goodness, she and Brody had made up from their fight.

"I live here. Where's Noelle, Ab?"

"You're not supposed to be here. You're supposed to be with Noelle."

Cam wasn't liking the way Abby was shaking the spatula at him. He liked even less the full-on scowl she had on her face. Something wasn't right. He felt his stomach tighten with trepidation.

"That's the plan, Ab. If you tell me where she is, I'll be with her."

Abby picked up a piece of paper from the counter and handed it to him. "She went to meet you, of course. Is she out in that weather alone?"

Cam scanned the note Abby handed him and swore. Noelle was out in the storm thinking he was going to meet her. She was being sent to her fucking death. She could die of exposure before they could find her. He felt the hair on the back of his neck rise in fear and anger. When he found out who wrote this note, he would enjoy beating the crap out of them. Slowly.

He threw the note on the table and tried to keep his voice calm for Abby.

"I didn't write that note, Ab. We need to get everyone together and get in the Jeeps and head out to look for her. We need to find her right away."

Abby's face paled, and her hand shook as she placed the spatula on the counter.

"You didn't write the note? Who would do such a thing? Oh God, Elle's out in that storm alone," she whispered.

He squeezed Abby's shoulder before heading to put his boots back on. "We'll find her, Ab. Don't worry. We have to find her."

He just needed to keep saying it. Abby picked up the radio and started calling Brody, Lucas, Caden, and Colt. Cam knew he would need everyone he could get to find her. Hopefully, she had headed straight for the clearing where she had been thrown. He grabbed his hat and pulled open the back door to head out into the storm.

"Stay close to the radio, Ab. We'll call you when we find her.

And we will find her."

* * * *

Boy, does this suck.

Noelle had finally decided she was well and truly lost. The sky was completely dark, and she couldn't tell north from south, or east from west. She was soaked, shivering, and scared. She was angry, too. She was getting tired of Montana kicking her ass. She needed to show Cam she could fucking take care of herself. He was probably out looking for her now, vowing to warm up her bottom since he had to rescue her. Again. This was the third time, and it was getting freakin' old.

She pulled on the reins and tried to take shelter under some thick trees, but the rain was coming down so hard they didn't help much. She dismounted and tied Poncho to a branch. She needed to wedge herself in between those trees if she could. It looked like she just might have some shelter if she could get in there. The tree trunks were close together, but she pushed herself back into the narrow space. It was uncomfortable, and she was still freezing, but it was a little dryer. She could actually keep her eyes open without the rain driving into them.

She wrapped her arms around herself, well aware if they didn't find her she could meet her death out here. She'd read in the paper about people dying from exposure in July, and it wasn't fucking July yet. Even if they did finally find her, she could get pneumonia and kick the bucket. *What a pathetic way to go.* She'd always pictured herself getting old and wise, passing quietly in her sleep. No way was she going quietly tonight. She had way too much to live for.

She heard a coyote howl in the distance and rolled her eyes. If the weather didn't kill her, the wildlife would. She looked around frantically as she remembered Cam telling her about rattlesnakes hiding in the brush. She hated snakes! It was so dark she couldn't see anything, so she pulled her knees up closer to her chest and rested her chin on top. Maybe if she made herself a very small target they wouldn't see her. Or hear her. Or smell her.

Oh fuck, I am so screwed!

Where's a taxi and a Starbucks when you need one? Noelle's stomach growled with hunger. It was past dinnertime, and hopefully Cam and the others had realized she was lost. They were her only hope right now. She shifted her weight and felt her cell phone bite into her flesh. She grimaced as she realized just how useless her cell was out here. She should have grabbed one of the satellite phones. She pulled it out anyway and peered into the screen. One bar. Not nearly enough to make a call.

Another gust of cold wind blew, and she huddled to try and keep warm. Unless she was found soon, she was in big trouble. She looked at her cell phone again and looked at the tall tree she was sheltering under. Perhaps if she could get to the top of the tree, she could get enough of a signal to make a call. She shoved her phone back in her pocket and drew a deep breath. She couldn't just sit here waiting for the weather or a wild animal to kill her. She had to do something.

She pushed to her feet and grabbed a branch. The bark and limbs were wet, and this was probably a very stupid thing she was doing, but she couldn't sit and wait for the grim reaper. Cam might not find her for hours. She needed rescuing now.

She dug her foot into a divot in the trunk and pushed while she pulled herself up to the first branch. She hadn't climbed a tree since she was ten, but she was pretty sure she could remember how. She stood on the branch and grabbed the next one she could reach, looking for a foothold in the dark. She found one and pulled herself to the next branch, stopping to catch her breath. She looked down and was surprised to find she was high off the ground. Perhaps her phone would work now. She fumbled in her pocket when she saw dim lights in the distance. They were coming closer and she could hear the hum of engines mixing with the rain.

Please let it be Cam.

She sat still as she strained to hear them coming closer.

This way. This way.

The lights got brighter, and the engines sounded louder. She gingerly moved back to the lower branch when she was flooded with lights. She hopped down to the ground, falling flat on her ass, and knocking the wind out of her. She waved her arms and started to push herself up when the Land Rover came to a stop. Poncho was clearly illuminated by the headlights, and her body was flooded with relief. If they found Poncho, they would know she was close by. She gave a yell as men exited the jeep, and they froze. She yelled again, and they turned and started running toward her. She tried to push to her feet, but her legs weren't working properly.

She looked up as the first man reached her and almost cried out with emotion.

Cam.

He'd found her. His expression was thunderous, but he scooped her up gently and carried her back to the Rover. He said something to one of the others, and just like last time, held her close all the way back to the house. He wrapped her in a blanket, but she was shivering, and her teeth were chattering. Even his body heat wasn't driving away the cold from the storm. She was chilled straight to the bone.

When they arrived at the ranch, Abby ran out. She'd obviously been crying. She pointed toward the stairs, telling Cam there was a hot bath waiting.

There was nothing sexual when Cam stripped her this time. She gritted her teeth against the pain as he lowered her into the water. The cold wasn't going quietly and it was only quite a while later that she was relaxed and breathing easier. Cam never left her side, only going to the bathroom door when Abby showed up with hot chocolate.

"Drink."

She drank gratefully, and it burned her stomach, but it felt good, too. It was good to be warm. She peeked through her lashes at Cam's murderous expression. He must be furious with her. Would he send her back home, telling her she was too much trouble?

"Cam, I'm sorry."

* * * *

She was sorry? What was she sorry for?

Cam knelt next to the tub and grabbed her hand. It was much warmer than only thirty minutes ago. He shuddered again as he thought of how they had almost missed her in the dark. It was only when they saw Poncho they realized they had, hopefully, found her.

"What are you sorry for, love? You haven't done anything."

Her mouth dropped open in surprise. "You had to rescue me. Again. This is the third time. I'm sorry I got lost and ruined your surprise."

Cam leaned forward and captured her full lips with his. He had to kiss her. He had come too fucking close to losing her. The crushing anguish he had felt in his chest as they had frantically looked for her would live with him the rest of his life. If he lost this woman, he was losing his heart.

Cam lifted his head. "You didn't do anything wrong. You shouldn't have been out there to begin with. The weather was going to turn bad. We knew the storm was coming."

Her brow knitted. "Then why did you have me go riding?"

Cam scraped his hand across his face. She was going to find out sooner or later.

"I didn't. The note you received wasn't from me. Where did you find it?"

"On the bed. What do you mean it wasn't from you? Who the hell has been in our bedroom and why would they send me out in a storm?"

She didn't look angry, only confused. Cam was sure anger would come later when the shock receded.

"I don't know, but we'll find out. As for the other times I've had to rescue you, only one was really your fault, that first time. These two are something different. I'll get to the bottom of this. I haven't done a very good job of protecting you, love. I wouldn't blame you if you took the first plane back to Florida."

Cam steeled himself for her response. He'd wondered whether this would be one thing too many. Being with him was one thing, but being with him and in danger was something completely different. What woman would stay when someone obviously wanted her hurt?

She reached up and traced his jaw with her fingers, leaving a trail of heat wherever she touched.

"I'm not going anywhere. Do I look like a quitter to you? No one is scaring me away from the man I love."

The band around his heart loosened. She wasn't angry or disappointed with him, and she wasn't leaving as soon as she could. She was going to give them a second chance. He started to pull his shirt off to join her in the hot, swirling water when he heard a knock at the door. He groaned with frustration. He wanted to be with Noelle right now. Just to hold her and know she was going to be okay. He pulled open the door and was surprised to see Julie there, pale and shaken.

"Cam, I think you need to come downstairs. We have to talk to you."

"I don't want—"

Julie placed her hand on his arm urgently. "You'll want to hear this. Abby is coming up here to stay with Noelle. Please, it's important."

Something in Julie's expression made him nod in agreement. He ducked back and gave Noelle a smile. "Abby's coming up here. There's something I need to take care of downstairs. I'll be back as soon as I can, love. I promise."

He headed out into the hall with Julie, passing Abby on the way up.

"So what is it I want to hear? I need to get back to Noelle."

Julie turned to him, her face covered in tears. Her hand flew to her mouth as she choked back a sob.

"It's John! Cam, John is the one who hurt Noelle."

Blood thundered in his ears, and he turned to bolt down the stairs, but Julie grabbed his arm with a beseeching look.

"Please, Cam, he's just a boy! Please hear him out. We don't condone what he did, but he's my son. He's my boy, Cam."

Julie was sobbing, and Cam felt his whole body tense, the emotions in him conflicted. He finally sagged against the stair rail and gave her a grim look.

"I'll listen, Julie. Because of you and Colt, I'll control my temper and listen. But this better be one hell of a good story."

Chapter Fourteen

Noelle was warm and cozy, tucked into bed, with a full tummy and her hunky cowboy stretched out next to her. She was also gobsmack surprised. Cam had just told her that John was the one who had been trying to hurt her. She was still trying to come to grips with the fact that a senior in high school she had only met weeks ago had tried to kill her.

"He wasn't trying to kill you, apparently. He was trying to scare you into leaving."

Noelle sat up and shook her head tiredly. It had been a long fucking day. It seemed like weeks ago she had been talking to her friends in her book meeting, but it was actually less than ten hours ago.

"Because of Gwen? Gwen convinced him to do it?"

Cam's cheeks were streaked with red. He was obviously ashamed of his nephew.

"Do you remember the day John went to help Gwen with her drapes? Apparently, she convinced John she was attracted to him. That she wanted to submit to him. She's a conniving bitch and didn't want to see me happy. So she lured John in with promises of a relationship if he helped her scare you into going back to Florida. The night we saw him at the restaurant he was there to meet Gwen. That's why they both tried to pretend they didn't see us."

"So it was John who shot the gun and scared Turismo?"

Cam nodded. "Yes, it was late afternoon, and he had just come home from school. Nobody would suspect John if he took off in one of the ATVs for a ride. He likes to blow off steam that way. He swears he didn't want to see you get hurt. He just wanted you to hate Montana and leave."

"He wrote the note?"

Cam pulled her close so she could feel the heat of his body and hear the beating of his heart.

"Yes, he wrote it. Gwen was pressuring him, telling him they couldn't be together if you didn't leave. He says he just wanted you to get lost out there by going for a ride in unfamiliar land. He swears he didn't know about the approaching storm. He was guilt-ridden and frantic when he heard what happened and admitted everything to his mom."

Noelle was still trying to make heads or tails of everything.

"He believed Gwen when she said they couldn't be together if I was here? What did I have to do with anything? And isn't she a little old to be attractive to John? He's eighteen for fuck's sake. She's old enough to be his mother."

"I'm going to let the swearing go since you've already been through more than enough tonight. Gwen's still an attractive woman if you don't know her too well and if she never talks or anything. John's heard about cougars so maybe this was his Mrs. Robinson. As for believing her, common sense has nothing to do with a horny teenage boy. He comes from a family of Doms, and he wanted to prove he could dominate a woman, and he wanted to get laid. He wasn't thinking too damn clearly until tonight."

She sighed and cuddled closer. "Un-fucking-believable. So what happens to John and Gwen now?"

"That's up to you, love. If we call in the Sheriff, Gwen will get in trouble, but so will John. Personally, I'd like to handle this inside the family. But, Colt, Julie, and I will understand if you want us to call in the law. Don't push me on the language, by the way."

"So much for giving me a pass tonight. How will you handle this? I don't want Gwen to get away with this, but I don't want to see John go to jail. He's just a kid."

"Ranch work is hard, honey. It can be the worst job in the world if you're given all the shit jobs on a ranch. Colt and I talked about it, and we think John should work from sunup to sundown, free of charge, seven days a week on the ranch, doing every messy, hot, terrible job there is this summer."

Noelle arched an eyebrow. "The sentence would be twelve weeks of hard labor? I like it. What about Gwen?"

"I've been on the phone with all the area clubs. She'll be persona non grata in every club west of the Mississippi by morning. The best punishment for her is to cut off what she needs the most. Pain. No Dom will go within ten feet of her from now on. She'll be shunned by the entire community."

"You've already done this? What if I had decided to call in the law?"

His arms tightened around her. "It wouldn't have mattered. I'm tired of Gwen messing up my life. From now on, she stays far away from me and my family. And most especially from you."

Noelle giggled and ran her hands up his chest. "Especially me, huh? You in love with me or something, you big, handsome cowboy Dom?"

He rolled her on her back, trapping her with his large, heavy body.

"Hell yes, I love you, Noelle. When I thought I might lose you, I was scared, really scared, for the first time in my life. You're everything to me."

She ran her hands down his muscular back, reveling in the feel of him. "I love you, too, Cam. So much. Promise me you'll always rescue me every time I get myself into a stupid situation."

"I promise, sweetheart. I'll always be here for you. I'm your man, and you're my woman. It doesn't get much simpler than that."

Noelle chuckled. "Nothing about this is going to be simple, cowboy. But you're worth it."

Epilogue

Noelle had been right. It wasn't easy. The last six months had been a blur of racking up frequent flyer miles, terrible loneliness when they were apart, and crazy, frantic sex when they were reunited. Even their week in Disney together hadn't been enough. It would never be enough. This was the man she was meant for.

She breathed a sigh of relief as she unpacked her last suitcase in the big bedroom she would share with Cam from now on. She wouldn't be returning to Florida to live. This was her home now.

Her darling waterfront condo had been sold to a newlywed couple, and her business had been transferred here. Cam had set up an area in his large office where she could work during the day while he was outside working on the ranch.

She and John had made a tentative peace. It had been one sad, pathetic young man who had begged for her forgiveness. She had cried with him as he told her how he had fallen for Gwen and had been willing to do anything to win her. They were working to build a relationship, and she was proud to see how hard he had worked over the summer. He had even decided to put off leaving for college this fall, to continue helping on the ranch.

Gwen had decided to move to New York City after she realized she was shunned from the BDSM community in this part of the country. Noelle couldn't help but be relieved she was out of their lives. She was only sad that it had come to something so extreme.

Abby and Brody's wedding had been beautiful. Noelle's parents had been happy for her and Cam especially when they found out he had a law degree. He simply smiled and said it came in handy when running a ranch of this size and complexity. Noelle had been shocked when he had revealed that little tidbit, but her parents now had an attorney in the family. Abby and Brody were deliriously happy and trying for a baby. She couldn't help but imagine the baby she might have with Cam. Maybe a little boy with Cam's dark hair and sky-blue eyes or a little girl with her red hair.

"I like that smile on your face. That means you're happy to be here. At last."

Noelle whirled around and threw herself at the sexiest cowboy that ever lived. He was all hers, too.

"I'm damn happy, cowboy. I hope you are, too."

Cam growled, pulling her closer. "Watch your language, sub. You get in bad habits when you've been away for a while. But I think I have something that will be a reminder for you."

He pulled away and reached into the nightstand. He held out the box with a twinkle in his eye. "Let's call it a homecoming present. Open it, pretty sub."

She loved presents and ripped the wrapping off in one tear, opening the box with a gasp of delight.

"Do you want to put it on?"

She couldn't get out of her clothes fast enough. The belly chain she had designed so many months ago lay in the black velvet, winking up at her. She couldn't wait to put it on.

He held it up, showing her the diamond-encrusted tag. "This says 'Cam's heart,' because you truly are my heart. I was only half living until I met you. This clasp is exactly as you designed it, love. Once I fasten it, the chain will only come off if it is cut off. Are you sure?"

Her heart pounded in her chest. She had never been more sure. Each time they were together, it only cemented their bond, not just as Dom and sub, but man and woman.

"Yes, my Master, I'm sure."

Cam's throat worked. He loved it when she called him 'Master', and his expression showed how pleased he was.

"You're my treasure, Noelle. I'll devote my life to caring for you, loving you, and protecting you."

His hands brushed her skin, leaving it tingling as he wrapped the slender chain around her stomach and fastened it with a click.

"Now you're mine. I love you, Noelle. I hope you love me as much."

He pulled her naked body close to his, the heat from him radiating and warming her.

"I love you, Master."

Cam shook his head. "No, not Master at this moment. Just Cam and Noelle. I, well, fuck, I just want to ask you a question. Aw hell, Noelle, will you marry me?"

Cam looked like he might pass out if she didn't answer him quickly. Her cowboy Dom was damn nervous she might say no. Not a chance of that happening.

"Of course I'll marry you. I love you, Cam. You rescued me not once but three times. There's magic in the number three, you know."

Cam lifted her and carried her to their bed.

"Three, huh? I can do better than that, sub."

She gave him a smile worthy of Eve. "Prove it, cowboy."

He pressed her to the bed, and she forgot everything but their love for one another, knowing it would be like this for the rest of their lives.

THE END

WWW.LARAVALENTINE.NET

ABOUT THE AUTHOR

I've been a dreamer my entire life. So, it was only natural to start writing down some of those stories that I have been dreaming about.

Being the hopeless romantic that I am, I fall in love with all of my characters. They are perfectly imperfect with the hopes, dreams, desires, and flaws that we all have. I want them to overcome obstacles and fear to get to their happily ever after. We all should. Everyone deserves their very own sexy, happily ever after.

I grew up in the cold but beautiful plains of Illinois. I now live in Central Florida with my handsome husband, who's a real, native Floridian, and my son whom I have dubbed "Louis the Sun King." They claim to be supportive of all the time I spend on my laptop, but they may simply be resigned to my need to write.

When I am not working, I enjoy relaxing with my family or curling up with a good book.

For all titles by Lara Valentine, please visit
www.bookstrand.com/lara-valentine

Siren Publishing, Inc.
www.SirenPublishing.com

Lightning Source UK Ltd.
Milton Keynes UK
UKOW031844150713

213846UK00018B/1654/P